PRAISE FOR

Cherry Girl

<u>Verdict</u>: ***Cherry Girl*** is a must read if you loved the rest of **The Blackstone Affair** series!! I have always wondered about this couple as we always saw glimpses of them throughout Brynne and Ethan's story but getting a play by play of how Neil and Elaina came to be from the start was... *SO. WORTH. IT!*

KAWEHI'S BOOK BLOG ~

This is a wonderful story, and any and all comparisons to the preceding books in **The Blackstone Affair** series are quite all right with me. :) Language, locations, alpha-guy, beautiful girl, sizzling sex...see, all good things to read more of! Neil is an enticing mixture of sentimental, considerate, responsible, and sexy! For *some* reason Raine Miller's dirty-talking British blokes are so fun to read! I'm looking at *Cherry Girl* like a surprise gift.

VARACIOUS READER BOOK REVIEWS ~

My final thought is that this is Raine Miller at her best. A true gem. You will laugh you will cry (both happy and sad tears) you will love, get turned on and ultimately, be completely consumed by *Cherry Girl*.

BOOK FRI-ENDS ~

I loved this story from beginning to end and every high and low in between!

BOOKIE THE BOOK CHICK ~

No need to say much other than...just a beautiful love story involving Neil and his *Cherry Girl* who are characters we met briefly throughout **The Blackstone Affair** series. I am a huge fan of Raine Miller...love her writing style. She has a way of making you fall in love with her characters. You almost feel like you know them personally when she's done.

KT BOOK REVIEWS ~

5 breathtaking stars!!! Once I started reading this book I was so hooked.... I just couldn't put it down! Simply magnificent. Just how the whole story unraveled was exquisite, a blast from the past and into the very present. Loved *Cherry Girl!*

L. HERNANDEZ ~

What can I say about *Cherry Girl* other then it is quite possibly one of the most beautiful love stories I've read. Raine Miller nails it again!

LESLEY DE WIG ~

When I finished this book I was speechless for words. The emotions, nostalgia, and the journey Neil and Elaina endured touched my soul. *Cherry Girl* is Raine Miller at her very best. Just when I thought she couldn't get any better, she writes this book that filled me with so much love and emotion. I just love their story. I felt as if I was there with them living every single moment, the good ones and the bad.

LUNA SOL ~

Cherry Girl is another beautiful story from Raine Miller. Beautiful and heartbreaking, but also heartwarming. It has everything I look for in a good love story.

WENDY LE GRAND ~

Cherry Girl

Other titles by Raine Miller

The PASSION of DARIUS
The UNDOING of a LIBERTINE

The Blackstone Affair
NAKED
ALL IN
EYES WIDE OPEN
RARE AND PRECIOUS THINGS

Cherry Girl

Cherry Girl

A BLACKSTONE AFFAIR NOVEL

RAINE MILLER

The author acknowledges the copyrighted or trademarked status and trademark owners of the following wordmarks mentioned in this work of fiction: Land Rover; Range Rover; London Underground; London 2012 Olympic Games; Jimi Hendrix; Bombay Sapphire; Schweppes; Djarum Black; J. Hendrix – *Wind Cries Mary*; Amazon Kindle; Lily Munster; Dr. Marten's; Chuck Taylor; UGG; Dolce & Gabbana; Guinness; Spotify; Burberry; Nurofen; Spiderman; Nike dri-FIT; JR Ward—*Lover Unbound~*

Cover Image
Cristina Cappelletti
© Dandyshadowplay – 2013
www.dandyshadowplay.com

DEDICATION

For my D who keeps me honest~

*Blossoms are scattered by the wind
and the wind cares nothing,
but the blossoms of the heart no wind can touch.*

—**Yoshida Kenko, (14th century) Japan**

CONTENTS

Cherry Girl

PART ONE

Elaina

*People who are meant to be together
will find their way back to each other.
There may be detours along the way,
but they are never truly lost.*

Author Unknown~

I remember the very first time I ever saw him. That first moment our paths crossed. The memory is branded into my head with indelible clarity. As clear as fine crystal with bright, sunlight shining through it.

I was ten years old when my brother, Ian, brought him home for dinner. He sat across from me at our family table. I probably looked like a total idiot gawking at him, but he didn't seem to mind my staring. Good thing, because even then I couldn't take my eyes away. Neil was beautiful to me when I laid my child's eyes upon him for the first time. Purely and simply beautiful.

It didn't matter that he was seven years older and totally uninterested in a gangly little girl with braces on her teeth who was definitely *not* anything close to beautiful.

He winked at me when he caught me sneaking a peek over a bite of Mum's delicious buns. I remember that gesture of his made me feel strange inside, like everything was squished together and turned to mush. Feeling shy and self-conscious, I tried to come to grips with the knowledge that I had met the boy I had every intention of marrying someday.

Yes, it's true. I fell in love with Neil McManus when I was a child. I am sure of how I felt, just as I am sure the feelings didn't go both ways. I watched him go through plenty of girlfriends over the years, too. What I don't remember is if he said anything to me that very first time we met. I do know he looked my mother in the eye with respect, and thanked her for the delicious dinner. That impressed me, even then. Even in my ten-year-old mind, I could read in him the deep appreciation he had for what Mum had easily offered to a guest in our home. I could tell that Neil was not accustomed to cozy dinners at the family table. He appreciated something I took for granted every day. He was just a young friend my brother had dragged home from God knows where, and from whatever trouble they'd been deep into, but he became something more than that from the very beginning. At least, for me he did.

Neil showed up for dinner quite often after that first meeting. Some days it felt like he was my new brother who'd just moved in with us. Other times, he'd show up after a few weeks' absence, wearing a hollow look in his dark, dark eyes. His home life was shit, apparently. No mum, just a dad of some sort who didn't care about him. My dad wasn't around a great deal either, but it wasn't because he didn't want us, it was because he travelled a lot for his job. I missed my father, of course, so I suppose it was natural for me to connect with an older male figure who was always nice to me, and didn't act like I carried the plague.

Neil called me *Cherry Girl* due to the colour of my hair. I'd have to agree with him on that. My hair was pretty much the colour of one of those dark cherries—nearly black with an undertone of deep red running through it. Neil told me my hair was very beautiful, and that small gesture was enough for my self-confidence to blossom. I took his compliment and ran with it.

I remember when he touched my hair for the first time, too. The memory is as perfect as the day it happened and I couldn't forget if I wanted to. Because it was also the first time he rescued me...

The cricket field stretched out to meet the forest edge a fair distance back. When I was eleven, on a summery Sunday afternoon, I had been sitting on the fence watching the local team play cricket. Neil and Ian were there too. I'd seen them strolling through talking to girls and other friends they knew. I was content to watch the match from my perch on the fence and blend into the background. The warm day brought out the crowd and space had become a premium, I guess. When a noisy, obnoxious group came through, being so small, I just got swallowed up in the melee that resulted.

A disputed call by the official started the ruckus. Then a fight broke out in front of me with two blokes pounding into each other, with no regard for who they might include with their misfires. I didn't duck out of the way fast enough, and was shanked by a fist that relieved me of my front-row fence spot. And right onto my left forearm, which managed to find a large rock to land on. Lucky me.

I heard the crack of bone, felt the pain, saw the brutal blows of the two brawlers, and smelled the beer that'd been sprayed about when the first punch was thrown.

I clutched my arm and tried to breathe, crying through the pain, sure that nobody would ever see me, let alone help me out.

I was wrong, though.

The sweetest sound was Neil's voice in my ear saying, "I've got you, Cherry Girl, and you're going to be just fine."

"My arm hurts," I told him through the tears.

"I know, darlin'."

"I heard a noise…like something snapped. Does that mean it's broken?" I wailed.

He picked me up and shouted something to my brother, the anger in his expression darkening his eyes to a frightening black as he eyeballed the two who'd caused my injury. I wouldn't want to be either one of those idiot blokes, confirmed by what I found out a day later.

Neil stroked my hair and sat with me until the doctor could cast my arm. And then, when he actually set the bone. The bone setting hurt, but the gentle reassurance and soft touch of Neil's hand on my hair almost made it cancel out. "Look at me, Cherry. Keep your eyes on me," he'd said with a smile, his hand moving slowly down my head over and over.

The next day, Neil brought some visitors by my house. Armed with humility and the telltale evidence of a second round of beatings, courtesy of Ian and Neil, the two fools responsible for my broken arm arrived with flowers and apologies for me and my panicked mum. My dad had a go 'round as well with them when he returned home from his business trip. Poor bastards didn't stand a chance, and it was safe to say they were scared straight onto a much more righteous path after that.

Neil's actions with me, in my time of need, cemented his place in our family for good. He basically became a second son to my parents and everyone seemed to understand and settle into this knowledge. I had to accept that Mum and Dad loved Neil too…which meant I had to share him with everyone in my family.

I wouldn't even let my best friend sign my cast until Neil did first. My knight in shining armor.

Back then.

When I was fourteen, and he was twenty-one, he joined the army and went away to fight for Britain. Mum and Dad had a goodbye party for him, and I remember how it seemed totally normal that we threw the going-away celebration for him and not his own family. Not that they had ever shown an ounce of interest that we'd seen expressed. It made me sad to realize that I could not recall even a single conversation where Neil ever spoke about anything personal in all the time he was around our family. The information I did know about him had always come from my brother, Ian.

The Morrison family had claimed Neil McManus for their own, and that was simply the way it was going to be.

When it was time to say our goodbyes I got shy, struggling with the words I wanted to say, but knew didn't have a snowball's chance in hell of forming on my lips. I didn't want Neil to leave without a proper send-off, but I was also totally self-conscious like any young girl would be with an adult man she adored and thought walked on water. I also waited until his girlfriend Cora had gone to the loo. I didn't care for Cora much at all and surely wouldn't have her fouling up my coveted goodbye to Neil. I wasn't stupid, just at a disadvantage.

"So, Cherry Girl, don't go falling off any fences or getting into the middle of a bunch of sodding idiots brawling while I'm away, all right?" His dark eyes twinkled with teasing so that I couldn't help but return a smile as they swallowed me up.

"I won't."

"I'll have a hard time cracking heads all the way here from over in Afghanistan."

I looked at the floor and gulped down the lump that had suddenly formed in my throat. "Nobody will bother with me. They never do," I said.

He dipped his head to find my eyes, waiting for me to look up. "I think that's about to change, Cherry."

You're growing far too pretty for your own good. The blokes are going to be all over you and they'd better be nice. Ian's got strict instructions to keep the crowds of arseholes at bay and make sure I'm regularly updated."

I blushed to the roots of my hair and gathered the courage to give him my gift. "I made you something." I handed the small packet to him and waited while he opened it, his big hands moving the tissue paper carefully aside. "It's a bracelet," I blurted, "for luck…to keep you safe." I held up my own wrist. "I made one for me, too. It has the infinity symbol and two good luck owls…I'll say a prayer for you every day and this will help me to remember," I trailed off, feeling shy again. "Be really careful over there, Neil, I want you to come back."

He brushed over the black-braided leather with the charms I'd added and smiled before looking up at me. "I will," he said in a whisper. The expression Neil wore was different this time. Something I'd never seen from him before, at least not directed at me personally. His eyes seemed like they could be a little watery too. We were definitely having a moment.

He brought a hand up to my cheek and held it there for a moment. "Thank you." He slipped the bracelet onto his wrist and tightened it. "I'm going to miss you very much, Cherry…and I'll wear this, and be the luckiest bloke in the British Army." He held his wrist up to show my bracelet before wrapping me into a hug with his big arms.

"I'm going to miss you too, Neil." *And, I love you.* I breathed in the smell of him and held onto it, hoping he *would* return safely someday, that the war would not take him away from us forever.

I felt his soft lips against the side of my temple and got the squishy feeling in my insides again. I didn't want to pull away, but the awkwardness of my young emotions bouncing all over the place made me self-conscious.

"Don't you *ever* change, Cherry Girl. Stay just how you are right now. You're utterly perfect."

Those were Neil's final words to me before he left to be a soldier.

2

Nothing stays the same though, and I did change. A great deal. It's impossible for life to stand still and of course, it never will. Change is inevitable in all of us.

The year Neil joined the army was also the same year everything changed at home for my family. Hell, everything changed all over the world.

September 11 happened.

My father was on the flight that crashed into the Pentagon building in Washington D.C. during the attacks. He'd been there for business and on his way to Los Angeles when the plane was hijacked and taken down. One of the sixty odd British nationals to lose their lives on that fateful day. My father was ripped away from us and we would never see him again. I guess that was the moment when I passed out of childhood and left it behind me. The innocence of my prior life was gone. Forever.

Time to grow up.

The horribleness of that year was really clouded for me. There are some things I remember clearly that were insignificant at the time, and other things I should have memories of, but are just...gone.

Like Dad's funeral for instance. I know we had a service for him, I've seen the pictures in an album, but I don't remember a thing about it or being there, or who came to pay their respects, or if I even spoke to them. I have nothing but blankness about that day. However I do remember stupid things like what shoes I was wearing when we watched the news on television, and saw the pictures of fires and wreckage and crashed plane parts, that had taken my gentle and loving father from me.

My red Chuck's with black laces.

It's funny how our subconscious can hold onto some memories and not others. Like the letter that Neil sent to me personally, shortly after it happened. I remember that very well, because I still have it safe in a box with all my other precious mementos.

Dear Elaina,

There aren't proper words to express the depth of my sadness for your unbearable loss. I want to be home in England more than <u>anything</u> *right now, but it is out of the question for the time being. Your father was the best of men. He loved his wife and children and worked hard for you all so you could have a safe and comfortable life. He was a true man in every sense of the word. This mad world we live in could use a great deal more men like George Morrison in it. He will be greatly missed. I wish so badly that I could be there for you and Ian, and your sweet mum right now. Please know that I am thinking about you and sending my love to you all. You are never far from my thoughts, Cherry. Don't you ever forget it.*

Yours always,
Neil

His letter was written hastily on military-issue stationary, which spoke to the hectic pace the army was keeping right after the attacks. Neil was busy fighting a war against terrorism and I was busy trying to grow up, and attempting to accept the fact that I had only one parent left in my life. Ian was busy at university and his career in law. Our mum was busy drowning her grief in glasses of gin.

We were all very, very busy getting on with our lives and doing our jobs. Isolated. Alone.

My dad had done well by us though, and there were settlements from his life insurance, the airlines, and the US government, so money was not the issue. No, it was more so the void and abruptness that we were forced to accept that he was never coming back to us.

Never.

I understood the finality of death then, and took my newfound knowledge to heart, closing off a little of myself, in an effort to prevent such terrible hurt from ever happening to me again.

Foolish, foolish girl.

My mum has always loved to cook. She still does, and just like that very first night when Neil joined our family for dinner, she embraced him as a son whenever he was on leave from the army, with huge home-cooked dinners. It was a given that he would come to see us, but now when Mum cooked in her kitchen, a hi-ball glass of gin and tonic stood at the ready to see her through. I cannot fault my mother. She was still a good mum and devoted to my brother and me with all her heart, she just wasn't as "present" or aware of my activities following the tragedy, as she normally would have been.

I had the open road of freedom dumped in my lap at a time when I needed censure.

As a confused and grieving teenager, I embraced the opportunity. Hell, I grabbed onto it with everything I had and then some.

By the summer I was seventeen, I had experienced just about everything you wouldn't want your teenage daughter doing. Yes, that was me. Parties, alcohol, smoking…boys. I sampled just about everything, and came out of my experience a little older, somewhat wiser, and a lot insecure about myself, and with no idea about what I wanted for my life. Well, I knew one thing I wanted.

Neil.

I still wanted him.

And Neil *had* been right about one thing.

The boys *were* all over me as I matured. I think he would have wished I was more selective in who I allowed to be "all over" me. Actually, I *knew* he wished I were more selective. I noticed the hard looks from him whenever he was home on leave, evaluating my boyfriend of the moment, his dark eyes ever watchful. The fact that he paid any attention to me at all was both wonderful *and* the bane of my existence. He was taken, you see. Neil had a girlfriend that just wouldn't let her claws out of him.

He would never look at me as a woman while she was wrapped around his cock. That was what I believed, anyway.

I had run through a slew of guys since he first went off to war, while Neil had stuck with Cora and been her loyal man. Why, I did not know. I couldn't stand her and knew she messed around with others, blatantly behind his back, whenever he was deployed. I often wondered how he couldn't see right through her. Or if he did see, and just didn't care. I figured his mates had been telling him what she was doing when he wasn't around. Ian had to know and should have told him, I reasoned. Was Neil with Cora just for the sex? Ugh. I hated to think about them together, and at the same time, I tried to forget about him. Forget that he would never belong to me. Forget that our time could never come. Forget about ever having the man I loved all for myself.

The following summer after I finished school, was when we crossed over into a new and strange territory together. The "ringing" of our proverbial bell came to pass, as it were. The spark that started a flame, that started a blaze, that started a forest fire, that would leave burns and scorch marks in its wake? This became part of our landscape.

Neil came home on a leave from the army that summer. When I was still eighteen, and he was twenty-five. That was the time when it finally happened for us…

3

I saw Neil in the pub when I went in after classes one evening.

Despite my destructive choices, I'd somehow managed to escape without too many bumps and bruises along the way. I don't know how I never got arrested, or pregnant, or worse, but I was very, very grateful for my good fortune. Or mostly, I realized my random luck for the miracle it truly was.

Somehow, I'd finally gotten my act together enough, to figure out what I hoped would be my "calling" in life. It appeared I had been blessed with a knack for languages. And my studies in French and Italian were helping to figure out what I'd like to do with my skill. I'd applied to go abroad as an *au pair*, working my way across Europe, with families who needed care for their young children, while I honed my studies in the local language. First on my list was Italy, then France, and maybe if things worked out, eventually I'd get to work in Spain and Germany too. I desperately wanted away from home and to be on my own. So this was my naïve plan to make that happen.

Neil had been on a leave for nearly three weeks when he showed up at the pub alone one night, looking like a beautiful golden god in his jeans, black T-shirt and black Doc's. Simply clothed, but perfectly gorgeous in his skin, miles of soldier-hardened muscles filling out the clothes as elegantly as a male model would. Emphasis on the "male." Neil was all male strength and power, and commanded respect just by how he moved in a room, military service notwithstanding. The size of him didn't hurt others' impressions either. He was a large man, tall and muscular where it counted, yet he was noted by all—male and female—both for his physical presence and his strong character. Watching him converse with acquaintances who wanted to catch up and express their admiration for his service in the army, I saw easily how people held him in great esteem and respect. In contrast, his young life had been so very different—so devoid of anything resembling the praise he was receiving from the citizens in the pub—that I was happy for him. It was right and proper that everyone noticed Neil McManus, because he very much deserved it.

The subtle confidence in his manner, the purposeful movements as he talked to people, the sound of his voice, all made me insane with wanting to be close to him, to put my hands on him. I craved the right to be able to touch him and have it be welcomed. I would have sold my soul to the devil to see him looking at me with something other than big-brother-is-only-here-to-keep-you-from-harm, little girl.

I had been drinking for an hour at least when he pulled up beside me and ordered a beer. The troubles with my boyfriend of the moment, Denny, had put me in a foul mood. He'd called me earlier, begging me to come down to the pub and meet him so he could "make it up to me." Whatever that meant, since we were so finished. Yeah, finding Denny shagging some blonde tart in the alley behind the pub, had pretty much put the death knell in our relationship, and I knew I'd never trust him again.

I don't even know what I was thinking by going there to meet him, anyway.

Denny was all kinds of trouble and he'd scratched that itch in me to be a rebel, I suppose. He was a young man with a dad who had a bit of brass. Enough to keep him flush with money and a flashy motorbike, and all things superficial that didn't really matter at all.

Things that made Denny the polar opposite of Neil in terms of character.

He hung with a cycle gang of sorts that dabbled in the illicit and illegal. I'd simply pretended to be unaware, but I was pretty sure Denny was dealing drugs as a side business of his main one—that of being a spoilt prick. If my father were still alive, I wouldn't have ever hooked up with Denny, or probably with any guy for that matter.

I'd most likely still be a virgin. An innocent. A pang of guilt and sadness washed over me at the thought of my dad. I missed him still…so very much, and knew he would be sorely disappointed in me if he could see where I was, and what I had been doing.

If I was honest, Denny's betrayal didn't really hurt me as much as I let on with him. I hoped to have a place in Italy by summer's end, and if everything worked out, Denny Tompkins would be just another memory from my rebellious past, that could fade away with very little bother to me.

I wanted out of England and to forget about all of the things I couldn't have, and all of the things I'd done.

I had Neil sitting on the barstool just beside me but nowhere close enough for what I desired. *Not fair.* I took a huge gulp from my glass.

"Don't you think you need to slow it down, Cherry?" he asked in his quiet way, managing to sound direct even though he spoke softly.

"Why should I? I'm not bothering anybody." I gave him a thorough look and inhaled, catching a whiff of his manly scent that did more to hasten my drunkenness than the wine I kept pouring down my throat.

"That's not true."

"Why, whatever do you mean, Neil?" I stared and watched him for a reaction, my curiosity piqued.

"It bothers me seeing you unhappy and getting drunk at the bar. It bothers me a lot." He narrowed his eyes a little and dragged those nearly black beauties back and forth in an effort to read me.

"What makes you think I'm unhappy?"

He swept a hand in front of me. "This is supposed to look like happiness?" He gave his head a shake and took a pull off his beer. "I don't think so, Cherry."

"I was waiting for Denny to show up and apologize," I confessed, mimicking his hand gesture toward my own body, "but he's probably off shagging the same twit from last time behind my back. Who am I kidding? These things happen." I shrugged at Neil, hoping he was getting my veiled reference to his totally unsuitable girlfriend, Cora, loud and clear.

"You need to lose that fool. I don't like him. Why even let him near you? You're better than that piece of news, Cherry."

"Don't call me that anymore." I pegged him with a hard look. "Why do you allow your piece of news near you?"

"Cora?" He looked surprised at my question, a slight smile reaching his mouth.

My stomach in knots, I grew reckless with my tongue and let it all out. "I can't have the one I want, so I guess I settle for sloppy seconds and get pissed in the pub when even that doesn't work out." I let my ugly words sink in for a moment and then delivered the sucker punch. "Your turn, *Neil.*"

He stared at me then. His eyes moving slow and purposeful, like a caress. It was as if he was trying to bring more confessions out of me by force of will. It nearly worked too. His beautiful dark eyes held the power to make it happen when he looked at me like he was at that moment. *Does he know how I feel about him? Has he always known? How could he not know?*

Those soulful eyes just about managed to pull the dreaded trifecta of emotion from my lips—just, but not quite. I only thought the words in my head. *I love you.* I was drunk and he was right there with me, acting as if he really cared. *I love you.* And then, I was left with the unbelievable idea that Neil *didn't* know. How could he be that unaware? How could he not know how I felt about him? *I love YOU, you idiot man.*

I'm guessing he truly didn't know after all, because he didn't take my bait.

"Cherry, I know all about what Cora's been up—"

"—I *said*, don't call me that anymore. I hate it now!" I spat angrily, signaling the bartender for a refill. I felt immediately guilty for lashing out at him, but it hurt too much to want him to see me as a woman instead of merely as a little sister who needed protecting.

Neil stood up and waved the bartender off, tossing down some notes to pay. "You're done here. I'm taking you home."

"Oh, you think so, do you?" I crossed my arms beneath my breasts and stared him down as best I could. I suddenly felt hot and more than a little dizzy.

His mouth quirked up at the side and then branched out into a cocky grin. "I *know* I'm taking you out of here, sweetheart." He took me by the hand and pulled.

"No, Neil!" I dug my feet in and balked against the force of him. It wasn't easy resisting his size and strength. I think inappropriate things at terrible times and was suddenly desperate to know what he would feel like on top of me. He was huge and I was on the small side. Would he swallow me up with his big body? I'd be very willing to find out, of that I was certain.

His eyes flared at me when he turned back to stare. If I wasn't mistaken, Neil was really looking at me for once. He swallowed hard, making his Adam's apple slide along his throat. I wished I could put my lips on his throat and keep them there. I was annoyed with him and secretly intrigued by his attentions at the same time. *Hell, he was so damned gorgeous.*

"You're so beautiful when you're spitting mad, *Cherry.*" He emphasized his nickname for me with a confident smirk, his eyes owning me. "Beautiful and utterly perfect."

You're utterly perfect…

I'd heard him say those words about me before. I wondered…was it even possible for him to believe such a thing? No way, right?

"You're beautiful too, but you're being an immensely arrogant arsehole right now."

"Is that so?" He leaned forward just a bit, putting himself into my space.

I hiccupped and nodded, feeling dizzier than I had moments before, instantly intimidated.

"You're out in the pub at night pissing drunk." His jaw ticked. "I'm not leaving you here, Cherry."

God damn, he said it again, and I just lost it. "And, I told you *not* to call me that anymore!" I took a step, stumbled on the chair rail, right into his hard chest. He steadied me against him and I had to resist the urge to bury my face in his shirt. It was damn hard not to. I really *needed* my nose buried in his shirt so I could memorize his scent.

"Okay, okay, settle down, girl. I won't call you Cherry anymore if you hate it so much, but only if you let me take you home. You need your bed."

He brought a hand up to the back of my head and stroked down my hair. And he could've called me by the name of any fruit in the world right now...apple, grape, kumquat, banana...and I'm fairly sure I wouldn't have even noticed, because he was touching me. Neil had his hands on me.

No, I need your bed. I lifted my eyes to his, my palms were flat on his chest, and I felt his heart thumping under my fingers. He focused on my mouth, and for a moment I got the feeling he was thinking about kissing me. My heart pounded so hard I'm sure my body must be moving from the force of it.

"Who do you want that you cannot have?" he whispered carefully, his eyes searing and dark, begging me to say. If I wasn't so stubborn I might have spilled my guts right then and there, telling him every single detail of every nice thing he'd ever done for me growing up, and how I didn't remember a time when I didn't love him.

I shook my head at him, feeling tears beginning to wet my eyes.

"Tell me—"

I inhaled quickly and turned my head away, just in time to see Denny step into the pub and lock eyes on me. "Oh God," I moaned.

"Baby, you came," he said, rushing over and trying to pull me into his arms. Denny's relief at seeing me waiting at the bar for him, was clearly apparent on his arrogant face.

"No, Denny, don't." I had just put my hand out to keep him off me when Neil stepped up.

"She doesn't want to talk to you anymore, Tompkins. Leave off her." Neil glowered down at my ex with a look of such loathing that Denny wasn't the only one surprised by the open hostility. Neil looked like he could make Denny bleed and would enjoy the hell out of ensuring that there was a big puddle of the stuff once he was done. I couldn't believe what I was seeing. Neil was behaving as if he were jealous of Denny.

I had to be incredibly drunk and my thought processes impaired. Why would Neil act like that over me and some bloke I'd already dumped?

"Elaina? Please baby, just listen. That tart meant nothing to me—" Denny ignored Neil's directive and tried to reach for me again.

I realized then, that my former boyfriend was as

incredibly stupid as I was drunk.

"Obviously your life doesn't either, you ignorant prick." Neil blocked Denny's attempted grab for me, stopping him cold. "You're not a very good listener, Tompkins. I told you she doesn't want to talk to you anymore. Get. Lost."

As Denny and Neil squared off, a wave of nausea so overpowering took hold of me, and I knew I'd be hideously sick. I clamped a hand over my mouth and slammed myself toward the loo, so incredibly grateful the door wasn't very far away from the bar. Both men let me go.

Thank God for the little blessings.

As I heaved over the toilet, expelling all the wine and happy-hour veggies I'd consumed while drowning my sorrows, I pined over my pathetic love life. How utterly revolting, wretched, and pitiful was I. A guy who cheated, and one who saw me only as a little sister. Fuck my life.

Once I was done puking, I made my way to the sink, where I leaned on it with both hands, panting into the mirror, and gathering the strength to splash some water on my face. Neil beat on the door, and barged in a second later looking fairly dangerous. In contrast to me, looking like shit.

The scowl on his face told me he was not in the least bit happy with me. But despite his opinions, he didn't lecture or fuss, he just pulled out some towels, wet them, and pressed the wad to my face. "Hold that to your head. I'll be right back."

"Denny?" I asked weakly from behind the towel.

"Gone. That fuckin' twat won't be bothering you again." I heard his heavy footsteps retreat and then the door of the loo shut with a click.

I groaned in my misery and tried to breathe, thinking if I could just crawl into a corner somewhere private, I could lick my wounds in peace. Tearing the wet towel off my face, I looked around the small room for the best covert access. I seriously considered hopping out the window as a means of escape. How could I ever face Neil again after this debacle? Embarrassed didn't even begin to cover what I was feeling.

"You'll be leaving out the front door tonight, darlin', and not the fuckin' window." I whipped my head around to see he'd returned with a glass of water for me. He was still wearing that frown too.

"I wasn't going to," I said meekly, mortified he'd read my shame as if it were a newspaper headline.

"You were thinking about it, though." He brought the glass to my lips. "Here you go. Little sips." His kind attentions overwhelmed me to the point I had to close my eyes. I just couldn't look at him anymore and keep myself together. I sipped the water instead and let him tend to me.

Selfish of me, I know.

"Better now?" he asked hopefully, in that low tone I recognized since as long as I could remember. I loved the sound of Neil's voice and I always had. Listening to him talk was a beautiful sound to me. Strong, but gentle. Soft, yet firmly convincing.

I nodded weakly, wishing I could slip through a crack in the floorboards so he couldn't see me in such a pitiable state. Why was he hovering? Shouldn't he be busy with Cora grinding his soldier's edge off?

"Why are you doing this, Neil?"

He ignored my question and frowned at me instead. "Let's get you out. You're so finished here for the night."

Then he put his hand at my lower back with a firm touch, and steered me out of the pub, completely taking charge of the situation.

I was far too weak to put up any sort of fight and I loved the feel of his hands on me, anyway.

Even if he were just being the concerned big brother tonight, I'd take what I could get. Any little bit of Neil was better than no Neil at all. I am not stupid.

While leaning against the window of his car, I welcomed the cold glass pressing into my temple, hoping it might cure my scrambled head. Not very effective though, when I could smell his deliciousness right beside me.

Neil just drove and stayed quiet. He wasn't a talker anyway. He spoke if he had something to say, and I got the feeling he really wanted to say something to me, but

I'd forced things to become so awkward between us, he probably didn't know how to begin. Nor want to. I felt like a complete and utter mess. Scratch that. I was most definitely a complete and utter mess.

I offered the first olive branch.

"I'm—I'm so—sorry for ruining your night with…Cora—"

He snorted at me. "I wasn't there for Cora tonight," he said, shaking his head.

He wasn't? This was news to me. As much as I wanted to hope, I forced my fluttering heart to calm. "You weren't there for Cora tonight." I said the words slowly and deliberately, an edge of questioning sarcasm in my tone that asked the burning but unspoken, *then why in the hell were you there tonight, Neil?*

"Nah, I wasn't." He looked over at me, his expression giving nothing away.

It was apparent he wasn't going to tell me why he *was* there either and the realization annoyed me greatly. "So, if you know about Cora, then why do you stay with her? She's running around on you as soon as you go away. She's a cheater. Every time, Neil. She doesn't love you like I—like—like she should do!"

Oops.

The silence in the car screamed in the small space between us.

"I'm not with Cora anymore."

"You were when you first got back. I saw you with her more than once."

He narrowed his eyes. "But, I'm not with her anymore, Elaina," he said with a bite.

"Really." I couldn't say much more, I was so surprised at his declaration. Neil and Cora were finished? If I wasn't sitting in a car and felt better, I might just jump up and do a jig in celebration, but my head continued to pound, and my stomach continued to storm.

"Really, there's nothing there," he sailed right back. "I've known for a long time what she gets up to and it doesn't matter anymore what she does when I'm away." He turned his head slowly to me, taking his eyes off the road. "We were just using each other from the get go…"

We were just using each other? Lovely. Picturing that twat getting even five minutes of Neil's attentions made me insane with jealousy. Images of him and Cora making love, touching each other, kissing passionately, flashed through my head until I couldn't help but groan against the cool window of his car. "Oh…I didn't know."

"Well, now you do."

Insane jealousy wasn't the only thing I felt either. There was also the violent urge to be sick again.

"Pull over!" I managed to sputter.

The second round was mostly just a lot of mortifying gagging and retching. There was nothing in me now except for the water I'd sipped. Neil didn't say anything once it was over. He kept quiet, bundled me back into his car, and drove us away. I closed my eyes and let him take care of me sure this was all a nightmare I would eventually wake from.

In the morning, I would deal with facing up to the spectacle I'd made of myself in front of Neil tonight.

I would pretend it had all been just a dream...because that was the most my poor heart could manage to do.

5

I could smell him again. The scent in my nose was so wonderful I didn't ever want to leave where I was in my beautiful, Neil-scented dream. I opened my eyes and saw darkness and unfamiliar surroundings...and him.

Neil was on his side watching me in the bed. Well, more specifically, in his bed.

"Wakey, wakey," he said softly with a smirk to go with it, not more than two feet from me.

I bolted up fast and found the blinking glow of the clock. *12:45 a.m.* "I—I—I'm at your flat? Mum will be—"

"—Just fine." He cut me off smoothly. "I rang your

house and talked to your mum. She knows you're with me so you can relax. How do you feel? Any better?"

I brought both hands to my head and rubbed, realizing I was missing my dress as I sat up in Neil's deliciously smelling bed. Bra and knickers only. I turned my head slowly to look at him in the dim light. "You undressed me?" I couldn't imagine the scenario of what that must have been like, and was again annoyed with him, because damn it all, if Neil was undressing me, then I sure as hell wanted to be awake when he did.

He nodded and then gently tugged me down to where I'd been positioned when I'd first opened my eyes. I settled back into my side arrangement and focused on him.

I decided to wait for him to explain. No need for me to start blabbering out a bunch of nonsense if I didn't have to.

"You fell deeply asleep after you were sick the second time. I carried you in and when I laid you down I could see your dress was spotted with…ah…puke…so I took it off you." I had to give Neil credit for keeping it cool because he kept his eyes on mine throughout that entire awkward explanation.

But, what he did share embarrassed me so much, I couldn't move, or speak. My mortification paralyzed me to the point I could only manage one thing. Cry. I did it quietly but the flood was unstoppable once it began. I couldn't take my eyes off him this time as they spilled over with tears.

"Don't cry, darlin', it's only me." He brought his thumb forward and brushed at my tears.

I just stared at him and kept crying. I couldn't look away and I couldn't stop my tears.

"Are you kidding me?" he said. "I got to see you in your knickers and watch you sleeping in my bed. I should be the one crying...in gratitude."

"Don't tease me. Please don't," I whimpered, holding up my hand, hating the sound of my voice and totally shocked at my predicament. *Surreal. Nearly naked and in bed with Neil after being sick in front of him twice and passing out.* I clamped a hand over my mouth. "I must stink to high heaven, and—and I need some water or something."

He helped me sit up again and handed me a glass from the bedside table along with two *Nurofen* tablets.

One, I was impressed with his forethought, and two, his total calm with me in the absurd situation. He said nothing while I downed the pills and sipped my water. He merely watched with that intense expression of his. I had absolutely no idea what he thought about all that'd been said and done between us since he showed up at the pub.

The covers slipped down to my waist, exposing me in nothing but a light blue bra, nearly all of me on display for him to see.

Oh, he saw all right. Neil's eyes roved over my skin and then flicked back up to my eyes and held them. It was impossible to know what he was thinking in that moment of supreme weirdness. I was unable to tell, and at a complete disadvantage with him. Was he repulsed by me? Turned on a little because I was nearly naked in his bed *and* he was a man? A soldier home on leave, and more than a little horny, in need of a woman? Did he even see me as a woman or just as a responsibility? Who in depths of hell knew? I surely didn't. Why had he picked me up and brought me to his flat in the first place?

"I can promise that you don't stink to high heaven, and are the prettiest wino I've ever had the pleasure of smelling in my bed." He sniffed in my direction. "Eau du Cabernet?"

"No bloody fair," I said pitifully.

"Sorry, that was awful." He brushed my cheek with his thumb. "I'll be good now, I promise." Another sweep of his fingers took the rest of my tears away before he set the glass aside and faced me again.

I dug deep for the courage to ask him what he was doing with me. I had to know or I knew I'd surely go mad. "What was all that tonight, Neil?"

He shook his head slowly. "I'm just in awe that you're really here." He reached forward again, this time entwining his fingers with one of my hands, until he gently held them suspended between us. "I can hardly believe it," he whispered. He stayed quiet for a minute, just holding my hand before he spoke again, his eyes carefully watching. "You never answered my question back at the pub, you know."

I gasped and shook my head, pulling on my hand to

unclasp it from his. "No, that was bloody stupid and I didn't mean it."

My efforts at resisting were completely pointless because Neil wasn't having any of it. He just gripped my hand harder. "Tell me, Elaina. Who do you want that you think you cannot have?" His voice was liquid soft and hard as steel, both the same time. I couldn't lie to him. Not when he asked me like this, face to face. The tension between us so raw, there was nothing to stop the hemorrhaging of my heart as it bled out all over Neil's bed sheets.

"You," I whispered, sure that my world was about to collapse in shambles once the truth was out there.

The most remarkable thing happened then. Neil closed his eyes for just a second, as if in relief at my answer, before bringing his forehead to rest against mine. We stayed like that for a bit, just the normal night sounds of London and the touch of our heads and hands, reminding me that this was indeed real and not a dream. My heart pounded deep in my chest, serving as another reminder that I wasn't dead and had just survived something miraculous.

A second miracle occurred when he nudged his head down and found my lips.

Neil kissed me.

We kissed.

I let him explore me, his soft beautiful mouth merging with mine, learning the feel of my lips as I learned his, gaining the experience of knowing what it was like to share the intimacy. His tongue was even softer, seeking entry in a gentle way but one I couldn't refuse either. I was aware only of us coming together and trying to ride the immense wave of attraction I felt for this man.

Neil took his time with our first kiss, but he could have taken me anywhere, done anything to me, asked anything of me. I would have been willing.

Nibbling on my lips in the softest way, tangling his tongue in with mine, he made me ache for more, and at the same time, want to weep in thankfulness that he'd finally come for me. *This is really happening.*

I don't know how many long moments passed before he stopped kissing me and pulled back. "Let me be the first to tell you that you were wrong." He stared at me, his thumb brushing back and forth at my cheek, his expression firm and solid.

It was my turn to close my eyes in relief this time. "I was wrong?"

"Dead wrong, Cherry." He nodded slowly, his eyes searing. "You may have me."

"What?" The ability to comprehend information had obviously left me.

"You can have me," he repeated, still holding my hand intertwined, his expression still burning into me with his dark, soulful eyes.

"But why—when did you know this—wait—you came to the pub tonight—you came tonight because…?"

"Because I heard you'd broken off with that fuckin' arse, Tompkins, and I was home on leave to actually do something about it for once. Do you have any idea how long I've been waiting for this?" His voice then had a definite edge to it. "For the timing to work out for *us*?" He sounded frustrated.

"You were waiting." I was in such disbelief I again repeated his words, trying to accept everything he was telling me. "You've been waiting..."

"I have." He leaned in toward my lips but didn't touch them. "Waiting and waiting forever. For you. Waiting for you to grow up. Waiting for you to see me as something more than just a friend of Ian's. Waiting for the right time to tell you how I feel about you." He whispered so close, I could feel the brush of breath from his beautiful words. "Just a very long time of waiting, Elaina."

"Oh..." I felt more tears threatening to spill.

"I don't want to wait anymore." His eyes melded into me and held on. "Please don't make me wait for you any longer," he pleaded. "I can't do it, Cherry. I just can't."

Such beautiful words. And they came from his mouth to my ears, about me...

"So tell me now, please." I took a deep breath and reached out a trembling hand to his face. I needed to touch him and feel the warmth of his skin. I needed to feel him in order to help my poor brain accept that this was really and truly happening in the moment—not some beautiful fantasy dream I would have to wake up from. It sure felt like a dream though. *Neil has been waiting for me...*

Here we both were talking about our feelings and wants and desires. Neil had me close enough to touch in his bed at his flat.

Truly unbelievable.

Again, I summoned my courage and asked, "I want to—no—Neil, I *need* to know exactly what you feel for me," I whispered. "I have to hear you say it to believe it."

He took hold of my shaking hand and brought it to his lips, his eyes never wavering from mine, and said the three words I'd dreamed about for forever, but never believed would come.

"I love you," he said clearly, just before kissing my hand again.

6

His declaration was soft and gentle in the way he formed his words, but so honest and clear at the same time. I believed he meant it. Neil had just told me he loved me and I believed him.

I felt my heart lose a beat—sure it'd just up and stopped working—when he'd said those three little words to me. Hearts will do that when under emotional duress or when something sad or terrible comes along. I think his declaration qualified as emotional duress. No sad or terrible anywhere in it though. Hearing those words from Neil was nothing short of glorious and perfect.

Neil loved me.

"Neil…I—I've loved you since I can remember.

There was never a time when I didn't." I looked to the side and gathered more courage to say the rest. "But then, there was never a time when I thought you'd *ever* feel the same about me, either."

"Look at me, Cherry." He took my chin and tugged me back to him. "You silly, beautiful, sexy, gorgeous, amazing girl, were once again, so very, very wrong about me and what I was feeling for you all these years. How could I not love you? You're perfect, remember? *Utterly* perfect. I just had to wait for the right time to tell you is all."

I listened to every word he said as he smoothed over my hair.

"Every time I was home, you'd have someone new and it wasn't fair for me to try to steer you away from them and into my arms."

I started crying again but this time it was mostly in happiness. "I wish you would've."

"No." He shook his head once. "No, I had to wait."

He took my face in his hands and brushed along the tears wetting my cheeks with his thumbs. "You're so beautiful to me, Cherry, even when you cry."

And then he kissed me like he had the right to. The way I'd always wished he might. Neil kissed away my tears and wiped out all of the longing I'd known for ages, all in an instant. I melted into his big body and savored his touch. His lips. His words. I had everything I'd ever wanted from him now.

"You were my Cherry Girl when you were little."

"I was." I nodded into his hands.

"And you're my Cherry Girl now."

"Yes," I managed another nod and just that one word.

"I love you, Elaina Morrison, and you'll always be my Cherry Girl. Always. Nothing will change it for me." He leaned forward and kissed me sweetly, whispering, "Believe me."

I couldn't speak. My ability to voice words had completely left me. I was so overwhelmed. All I could do was stare back. And breathe.

Neil tilted his head at me. "You look like maybe you don't."

"I do but I—I have to take a shower now," I blurted. "And use your toothbrush, and get something to wear. I puked with this mouth tonight. *Twice.* And I've got no clothes on."

He broke into a smile at my announcement, and didn't even flinch at my puke comment. He must really and truly love me.

"Please say I get to help you with all of that."

"The teeth brushing, maybe—the shower, no," I fired back, suddenly feeling shy about the direction this conversation was heading and my state of undress. In the sanctuary of my mind I could be bold about wanting to be with Neil, but it was too soon to just slide between the sheets together and start shagging. I needed to come out of my shock first before we got down to the sex part. *What if he wants it tonight?* How would he take the news when I told him I needed a little time to get to that point?

Turned out I had nothing to worry about because Neil was the perfect gentleman with me, as always.

"I know that, beautiful girl," he said, with a peck to my nose, "but you're staying here tonight, yes?" He swept his eyes over me again before landing on my face. The look he gave me was almost a look of pleading. I could see how much he wanted me to stay, just as much as I wanted to pledge myself to him.

"Yes." I nodded slowly. "I'm staying here tonight." I planted both hands on top of the sheets, one on each side of my hips, showing him I really meant it. "I want to be here with you."

"Good. That's all I need right now. I just want to hold you and know you're here, safe with me and that this—with you...is real." He brushed over my hair with his hand again. "I'm afraid I'll wake up and you'll be gone. I need to get used to the idea of having you all to myself."

Yes please!

The burgeoning shyness grew stronger until I had to look away. My eyes landing on the thin sheet barely covering my body didn't help me to feel extra confident either. I needed to establish some truths first.

"Okay..." God, I sounded like such a trembling idiot. "This...with us...it *is* real, right?" My insecurity rang out clearly in the tone of my voice. I breathed heavier as my heart pounded, waiting for him to answer.

"Yes, Cherry, it's real." He tugged on my chin with his index finger to get me to look up.

I could see the earnestness in his eyes, and in the way he studied me with his dark browns when I finally looked at him.

"Completely real." He took one of my hands and placed the palm over his heart. "Feel that while I kiss you," he said, before sliding behind my neck with his other hand and pulling me onto those soft magical lips of his, "and you'll know it's very real."

But this time, Neil was trying to make a point, and his kiss was more demanding as he tangled tongues with me. He plundered my mouth and I allowed him access. And I did feel his heartbeat under my hand.

I tried to memorize the sensations, because I couldn't bear the thought of forgetting how I felt with him at that moment.

When Neil finally broke away from our kiss he still held the back of my neck firmly in his hand, taking control of our moment together, and I loved it. He made me feel cherished and I wanted to float in the feelings for forever.

"Cherry, I love you. And I just need you to be here

with me. That's all I want. I won't ask you for more than that until it's right, and we both want it. We'll know when that time comes. And everything else will get itself worked out when we're ready. Okay?" Another slow and thorough trace of his tongue in my mouth had my stomach fluttering and my heart racing.

I managed to nod back and whisper, "Yes." I brought my hands up to hold both sides of his face. "I've loved you for as long as I can remember."

Then, Neil smiled at me. His entire beautiful face lighting up from his eyes to his chin. My guy looked really happy. *My guy. I have a guy. Neil. Neil McManus is my man now.*

Christmas and my birthday had come to me early this year, and both at the same time apparently.

Then I watched him get up from the bed and head into his bathroom. I heard the shower turn on and then the opening and closing of cupboards. He returned a few moments later with a big towel to wrap around me, and said he'd left me a shirt and some shorts I could wear after my shower if I liked. He told me he would be in the kitchen setting up the coffeemaker for the morning, and then he left the bedroom and closed the door.

I stayed in Neil's bed for another moment and did my best to take everything in. I was definitely a mess on the outside, but inside where my heart still thwacked out a beat, I was absolutely floating around cloud nine.

He loved me. Neil really loved me, but damn if I'd allow him to kiss me again before I got clean and comfortable. I felt utterly gross and hideous, and still had trouble processing all that had just happened with us in the span of a very few hours.

I left his bed and headed into the bathroom. The shower was already hot and steaming up the small space. As promised, he'd set out his toothbrush and paste for me to use, and even some silky boxers and a soft black T-shirt with *The Jimi Hendrix Experience* in white letters across the front.

I knew Neil was a Hendrix fan, and I'd even seen him wearing this very shirt on occasion, and yet the fact he'd picked it out for me in particular, touched me. I reached for it and buried my face in its softness, inhaling deeply. Neil's scent had always been heavenly to me and I'd been addicted to it for years. Hard to describe, but, absolutely lush on my sensibilities. Like fresh air, and forest spice, and pure water, all combined into the perfect blend of male fragrance.

And I'd been restricted from indulging in it for most of my life. But, not anymore.

I shut the bathroom door, stripped out of my bra and knickers, and got clean in my boyfriend's shower. *I so loved the words contained in that thought.*

I'm sure I wore a ridiculous grin on my face the whole time I scrubbed. Once I was done in his shower, and worked out my teeth with *his* toothbrush, I was still grinning stupidly into the mirror like an idiot. I was so glad the door was shut and Neil couldn't see how much of a lovesick fool I was being at the time. Pointless indeed. He would know it the moment I stepped out, anyway. He probably already did know.

Cherry Girl

I left the bathroom dressed in his T-shirt and silky boxer shorts. Better than naked in a towel or my puked-spotted clothes, and really sexy to have my skin against things that had been against his previously.

His shirt came down to the top of my thighs and I'd already decided I was keeping the thing. Yeah, Neil's beloved Hendrix shirt would forever belong to me. I had absolutely no qualms about my thievery either. I didn't want to have to be without the scent of him once his leave was over. I wouldn't have him for long before he had to go back to being owned by the British Army in Afghanistan. That meant his shirt wasn't getting washed anytime soon. If ever.

My inner ramblings distracted me to the point I wasn't thinking about what might be waiting for me when I came out. But the sight that greeted me upon my return to the bedroom in nothing but Neil's shorts and shirt, was not even close to what I expected. Stopping dead in my tracks, I'm sure my eyes were bugging out of my skull. The towel I'd been using to dry my hair slid from my grip and onto the floor with a soft thud.

Neil was in his bed, and he was waiting. For me. Definitely for me.

Holy Hell, he was a beautiful man. Sitting up against the headboard, he was leaning back, his wide bare chest exposed for my eyes to drink in. The cuts and angles of his hard muscles and golden skin, in contrast to the white sheets, nearly made me whimper aloud. I wanted to touch him so badly and knew there was a very good chance I would be getting my wish soon.

I could see that his nipples were hard. His gaze was trained upon me, deep with liquidity, mysterious and sensual, with a bit of an edge. I could only imagine what he was thinking about. Sweaty, crazy, naked shagging I'm sure. I definitely was.

My nipples were hard too, and I felt an involuntary shiver roll down my spine at the thought of Neil putting his hands on them.

I'd seen his body before. I knew what Neil looked like without his shirt on, and I knew very well about the washboard abs, and how they tapered into a V at his hips that made my insides a quivering mess whenever I was lucky enough to get a decent look at him. Which happened only on occasion, unfortunately.

Neil was blessed with an earthly form that easily put him into mythical god territory, but I'd never been in a position to allow myself to think of him in that way. Those times I'd seen him had been when he was working out with Ian or roughing 'round with boys at football or having a swim.

This situation was completely different. Neil was like this for me, and for me alone. He was offering himself to me—his body for my eyes to see, for my hands to touch, and for my lips to kiss.

"You've dropped your towel," he said softly, splaying a hand out over the sheet, making his forearm muscle flex.

"I know." I struggled to breathe through the pounding inside my chest and reached down for the towel.

"Leave it."

Neil's voice was harder, different—a command really. I froze mid-step, flipping my eyes up so I could see his face and understand what he meant.

His long muscled arms were stretched out toward me. "Come here, beautiful," he said softly. "Don't think about anything that scares you right now. It's only me...and you."

I nodded at him but no words would come from my mouth. All I could do was take in the experience of the moment and try to hear what he was saying to me.

"I want to hold you, and be close, and know that nobody is going to come between us or try to take you away from me. I want you all to myself for once." He tilted his head a little. "Do you understand?"

"I do," I managed.

Neil kept his arms out, his eyes glittering at me in a way I'd never experienced from him before. He was demanding from me, sure, but that's not what gave me pause. The feelings rushing through me were thrilling, but also very frightening at the same time. My emotions paralyzed me because I really understood, right then and there in that moment, the enormity of what I was doing. Giving myself over to another person. Giving myself to Neil.

It made me extremely vulnerable. Didn't it?

I felt the warning kiss of fear brush over my heart, as

clearly as a cold breeze that makes you rub your arms in an effort to ward off a shivering chill.

I didn't know how I'd survive if I lost him. If he stopped loving me, I wouldn't be able to bear it. Or if I lost him to the war, which was a terrifying risk all on its own—and one he took every day he remained in active military service—I'd never make it out intact. Losing Neil would destroy me after learning what it felt like to be loved by him, as I learned on that night.

"Don't think about the bad things, Elaina. Let all that go and come to me. My beautiful Cherry Girl…come over here and let me love you."

I went.

All I knew, is that I found my way into the strong arms that I never wanted to leave, that I would ache for once he returned to the army, and that held me so perfectly, I had to tamp down the urge for more tears.

Neil's hard body and soft lips pressed into me, allowing me to feel a little of how it would be with us, teaching me what it meant to be granted the deepest wish of my heart—to be loved by Neil McManus.

And at the very same time, I was forced to recognize my most terrifying fears in regards to Neil.

I could lose him.

And it would kill me if that ever happened.

7

Neil was careful with me once he got me into his bed. He didn't go beyond blistering kisses even though I would have let him. He kept us in check and his control was remarkable, because when he pressed against me I could feel how hard he was through his shorts. That it was Neil, and *his* erection I was feeling against my hip just made me hotter for him.

He hadn't come to bed naked as I imagined he might have when I first stepped out of the bathroom and saw him waiting for me. No, he was covered, plus the sheet was now completely bunched up between us from my restless legs flailing around. Good thing for the layers and the self-control Neil possessed, because I surely had none.

When things got too heated he'd pull away and just

look at me, stroking my cheek or my lips with a fingertip, waiting until we both cooled down.

I stared up at him in the dim light, my insides already a fluttering jumble to begin with, even more overwhelmed from his plundering kisses. I wondered where this was all going to lead with him.

Unable to keep still, I arched into him and then pressed my legs together to relieve some of the ache. "I—I need—Neil, I—"

"—I know exactly what you need, darlin'. I know what you need, just like I know what I want to do with you."

He shifted his hips into me so I got a good feel of what was going on with his cock. He felt huge and this was not a surprise in any way. Neil was a big guy all over. I couldn't keep my hands off him, either. I splayed out my hands across his back as I met his thrust with my own body, feeling heated desire swarm me. I would have done anything he was willing to do and knew that any slowdown of passion would have to be all on him. I extended my hand down the front of his shorts, slowly putting my hand over the rock-hard ridge filling them up.

Neil hissed as my hand came to rest over his erection, his own hand covering mine instantly. "But we're not doin' any of it tonight," he told me softly, gently taking my hand in his and moving them both to the side.

"We aren't?"

"No. Not here and not like this." He pressed his lips to the hollow of my throat and spoke against the skin there. "You're too precious to me for some desperate shag in the middle of the night." He moved up to my lips. "I won't do that to you. It'll be special when we make love. And we will." He murmured against my lips. "Oh yeah, darlin', we will, and it'll be very…very…good when we do."

Neil's strong arms held me enclosed within them, teaching what it felt like to be body-to-body with the man I loved.

Beautiful, wonderful, and perfect is how it felt.

We also found that conversations came easily for us. Made total sense considering we had years of shared experiences to draw from.

"Do you remember the first time you came over to our house for dinner?" I asked him.

"Of course." Neil's fingers stroked up and down my arm as if he just wanted the contact of touching me.

I couldn't get enough of his hands on me, either. His touch was an affirmation of sorts for me. It made everything real and I desperately needed to believe that this was. All my hopes and dreams were riding on that simple fact.

"I fell in love with you when you winked at me over the table." I looked into his eyes and saw the twinkling laugh reflected in them even if he was silent. Neil could communicate very clearly without speaking, and he did it all the time. I'm sure it was a good skill for the military too, especially when he was leading troops into battle. No wonder he'd already achieved the rank of captain in the British Army.

"I remember winking at you, thinking you were being so generous, offering me the last of your mum's gourmet buns."

"You were nice to me," I told him, "so I could afford to be generous. Not many seventeen year olds will give a ten-year-old the time of day, let alone secret winks."

Instead of responding to my confession, Neil loomed over me, his mouth dipping down to meet mine, his body pushing me back into the mattress again where he kissed me until I was breathless.

He laid his hand over my heart and held it there. Nothing sexual or wandering in the way he touched my breast, just the gesture of feeling the place where my heart pounded under the skin. "This heart is so beautiful, now as much as when you were ten. You have a beautiful heart, Cherry."

Just like you do, Neil.

"I think I used to," I said.

"What do you mean *used* to?"

I curled into his chest and traced a finger into the hollow of his throat. "After my d-dad died, I—I know I changed and I'm not—I'm not the person I was before. I'm not the nice girl you remember from years ago, Neil. I hope you know that."

"But you are," he said. "I know that's not true. Why would you even think such a thing?" He tightened his grip around me.

"I've done things I never would have, if Dad were still here."

"We all have, Cherry." He kissed me slow before speaking. "I wish I'd been able to be here back then. I worried so much about you after your dad was taken."

"I still miss him, so badly."

"Of course you do. That's normal."

"But he would be ashamed of me and what I've been up to these last years."

"And what's that exactly?"

I didn't know what to answer. If I was truthful, then Neil might be disgusted with me. If I wasn't, then it made me a liar by omission and I didn't think I could do that to Neil. I held our love to a higher standard, and somehow I knew he did as well.

"Well, I'm not innocent. I've done things I am ashamed of. I've messed around with a bad crowd and…boys. Dad raised me to be better, and to think more of myself than where I've been keeping company, and where I've been."

"If you're referring to that cocksucker, Tompkins, then I agree wholeheartedly—he wasn't fit to even share air in a room with you."

I laughed softly. "I know. Dad would never have let Denny in the door to look at me, let alone take me on a date."

"Your dad was a wise man," Neil said wryly.

"I was in a fair bit of shock back at the pub when you were defending me. I couldn't work out why you would be so interested...in me." My voice trailed off into the night time silence.

Neil's response was to roll me onto my back and kiss me with deep probing strokes of his tongue, almost harsh and desperate in his method to convince me I was worthy. "Have you worked it out now?"

"Not really," I answered shyly, "but I am so grateful you are...interested."

"Let me show you something." He slid open the bedside table and brought out a small object. "Hold out your hand, please."

I did, and felt him slip a bracelet onto my wrist.

"You kept it all these years?" I asked, feeling like more tears might pour from me if he kept going with the gestures. I held my wrist up so I could get a better look in the poor light. The bracelet I'd handmade for Neil as a good luck charm to keep him safe in the war looked a little battle worn but it was still intact, still with the two owls and the infinity charms I'd put onto it.

"Yes, I kept it all these years. You made it for me.

Hell, I wore it as often as I was allowed. It goes everywhere with me."

I could see the evidence of that easily from the texture and colour of the leather. I brought it to my nose for a sniff. I could smell Neil's scent on this small scrap of leather knots and brass charms, and knew it had lain against his skin.

"I still have mine, too," I said.

He drew me close into the curve of his arm and rubbed the back of my neck with his fingers. "You know that I think of your brother and mum as family more than my own?"

"They love you, Neil."

Again I could hear the ache in his voice. Neil didn't speak of his shitty family life, or how he'd been virtually on his own from far too young of an age. He wasn't a complainer, so for him to bring it up in a conversation with me felt monumental.

"I love them, too. And you all love me back, Cherry. I don't need anything more."

As I lay in the cradle of his arms, I looked up at the ceiling of his bedroom flat and thought about how happy I was in that moment, being cuddled in the bed with Neil and enjoying his soft caresses and slow kisses. Neil and me together.

"Oh my God, we have to tell them about us!"

He laughed. "We can do it tomorrow."

"Okay then. We will. I can't wait to see Mum's reaction."

"I'm more worried about Ian." He cupped a hand over his cock. "I'd like to keep this intact."

It was my turn to laugh at him this time. "I think your prized possession is safe enough."

"Thank bloody hell."

"Neil, you're forgetting the facts."

"Oh?" He raised a brow at me.

"Yeah, that fact that the Morrison clan claimed you long ago, and we're never giving you back."

He liked that. And kissed me for a long time afterward just to show me how much he liked it.

Later, we had an opportunity to talk a little about the others who'd come before. That part wasn't so nice, but needed to be discussed and I'm glad we did. I didn't want him under any illusions that I was an untouched virgin. I'd been with a few guys, and most recently Denny Tompkins, and felt he should know the truth. I saw the tightening of Neil's jaw as I got that off my chest, but still knew it had to be shared. He needed to know. My Denny was his Cora.

My only consolation was that Neil despised my former boyfriends just as much as I'd loathed him with Cora, and others over the years. I hated that bitch.

The most important aspect in all of this though, was how much we wanted to be together and needed what only the other could give to each of us. Now that we'd had a taste of how it could be, no other would ever do. For me, it was Neil...or nobody. He loved me in spite of my past and I felt the same for him.

We held onto each other our first night together, whispering in the dark, sharing our dreams and unburdening our demons. With Neil's arms around me, I drifted off to sleep peacefully. I knew that the scent of him was real when I breathed him in.

So much hope was riding on the future back then. I didn't imagine anything could take him away from me after such a hard-won victory.

Life wouldn't be so unfair to Elaina Morrison after all I'd already endured.

His love was something I never questioned on my part and I did have it. I can look back now, and say with complete conviction, that I definitely had Neil's love.

I had it for a short time.

Far, far too short a time.

I had Neil's love until fate swiped it away and took from me...again...until I was lost once more.

Alone. Once more.

PART TWO

Neil

Drifting on a sea of forgotten teardrops,
on a lifeboat sailing for your love.

Jimi Hendrix, Drifting~

8

That month with Elaina was the happiest time I could ever remember. I don't have many memories where I was truly happy. I lived for the day and got along the best I could. It's always been my way. But the time with her trumped everything else I'd known up to that point.

I'd known longing. Hell, I'd been longing for Elaina since forever so it didn't feel any different. I just had to wait on her for a time, and then...I got to be the luckiest man in the world when everything came together for us. I finally got my chance to tell her what she meant to me.

I had my girl, and she loved me too. We were together and we had forever to stay that way.

There were many things to learn about each other,

despite the comfort of being with a person you'd known for ages, and yet, there were still mysteries. I could spend my life discovering her and never grow tired of the journey. This I knew.

The first person we told about us was Elaina's mum. *Well, finally the two of you have sorted out what the rest of us have known from the very beginning* was the first thing out of her mouth, along with a shriek and hugs all around.

It was a wonderful thing having a family that wanted you.

Her brother, Ian, was next on the list to share our news. He was happy for us and showed a similar reaction as Elaina's mum but with a bit of *You shagging my little sister, now, mate?* thrown in with a challenge. I assured him as best I could, but…yeah, better if we two didn't discuss that part.

Well, I wasn't technically, but that would be changing. We couldn't keep our hands off each other, and the shagging would definitely be happening sooner rather than later, at that point.

The problem was, I didn't have a long time before my leave was up and I went back on another tour. There was a great deal of ground to cover in those few short weeks, and I wanted everything to be perfect when we were together for the first time.

I took Elaina for the weekend to the Somerset coast at Kilve. A fellow officer, I'd met in the SAS, had a sister who ran a bed and breakfast there. He'd mentioned the place to me on more than one occasion. Thankfully, when I gave Hannah Greymont of Hallborough Park a call, I was able to secure a booking. I was as sure of my plans away, as I was of my destiny...

"How did you find this place?" she asked in awe as we came up the gravel drive.

"One of my mates, a fellow officer in the SF, told me about it. Blackstone's his name. His sister owns the house with her husband. Pretty amazing isn't it?" And it was. The Gothic stone house in front of us was a country mansion that rivaled anything you'd see on the BBC.

"It's beautiful, Neil," she said quietly, "a perfect place to bring us."

She looked so gorgeous next to me, all graceful and fine in her blue dress and long sexy legs curved in the seat of my car. I had picked up on some vibes, though. My girl was feeling a bit shy and I had a pretty good idea why. I'd take care of that little problem just as soon as I got her alone in our suite, though. Very slowly and with great care. *Down, lad!* I really had to focus on the ultimate goal of this trip and what my purpose was. And it wasn't just to get her into bed, taking our relationship to the next level, although I'm sure it looked that way. It was bloody difficult to focus when she looked like she did.

"You're beautiful," I told her, "and I love you for agreeing to let me sweep you away for the weekend."

"Just for agreeing to come here with you?" She gave me a look.

Stupid idiot moron dickhead. "No, not just because of that. I love you all the time." I reached for her and pulled her against me, searching her face for clues. "Second thoughts?"

She shook her head, blue eyes bright and whispered, "Never." Elaina brought her hand up to my face and held it there. "I'd go anywhere you asked me to. I love you, remember?"

"I won't forget you told me that." And I wouldn't. Those words were precious words to me.

"Good. You'd better not forget."

I adjusted her against me and kissed her good and slow, until she was pliable in my arms, and I was thinking about beds and getting her naked, and a shit ton more inappropriate ideas for the moment.

"So, I have a plan here," I confessed against her ear.

"Hmm, thought so," she purred. "What is this plan you have?"

I pulled back so she could see me. "My *plan* is to get us settled into our room first." I tilted my head at her raised brow, sure she was thinking my motives were in the gutter. Well, they mostly were, but she didn't need to know that, and I hid it well. "And then…how 'bout I take my gorgeous girl to dinner where I can sit across the table from her and drown in her exquisite beauty? What do you say?"

She laughed at me. "Okay, I say yes to that."

"Are you laughing at me, Miss Morrison?"
"I believe I am, Captain McManus." She nodded through more giggling, and then pressed a sweet kiss to my lips. "You have a touch of poet in you, I fear. Better you don't let your troops know it."

"And I thought my little speech was well done," I protested.

"Aww, you can talk like a poet to me any time you want to, babe." She blew me a smiling kiss.

I shook my head as we made our way inside to registration. I had Elaina happy and glowing on my arm, yes, but thinking about how I had to leave her in a few short weeks—I had no idea on God's green earth how I was ever going to manage to do it.

Blackstone's sister, who told us to call her Hannah, put us in a lovely corner suite done in blue, that overlooked the sea from its windows. The view of coastline and lavender fields was superb, but seriously underappreciated by my filthy mind. Yeah, the only view I cared about was one of Elaina in front of it. Naked. That was the view I wanted to gaze upon. The only one that mattered very much.

As I stared through the glass, I realized I had it bad.

Elaina was rustling around in the bathroom setting out her things while I pondered the anticipation of what was finally going to be a reality after so long a time of wanting her.

But, I wasn't without some reserve over what we were about to do here in this beautiful stately house along the scenic Somerset coast. Elaina was an adult, but she was also considerably younger than me. Sometimes I felt guilty for wanting her when I probably should have picked a woman closer to my own age, but I'd learned a long time ago, that you don't get to choose who you fall in love with. They chose you.

For me, that person was a beautiful girl with cherry-coloured hair and dark blue eyes, and she alone held the sole key to my heart.

Just those few thoughts about her woke up my cock to the point where some discreet rearranging was required. Well then, we might really need the whole box of condoms I'd packed for us in my bag—

"Oh babe, you should see the view in here," she called to me from the bathroom, interrupting my shag logistics for the time being. Thank bloody Christ. As I went to her I chastised myself for the trepidation I felt the need to hide, trying to get past the idea of what I'd be doing with her, and to her, as much as I possibly could, in the limited time we had left.

Facts were facts. Elaina wanted me as much as I wanted her. Nobody here was underage, nor an innocent, either. That fact bothered me and then it relieved me, too. I wasn't the first man to be inside her but then I didn't have to worry about deflowering a virgin either—something I'd never done, and had no desire to experience. No, I had my girl, and she was all I wanted.

Elaina was an adult woman. We had the blessing of

her family who knew she'd stayed at my place overnight a few times already. They had to suspect. So, why was I feeling like a horny teenager about to sneak a shag?

"Are you coming, babe?" she called out to me again.

Oh yeah, darlin', I will be and so will you.

I stepped into the bathroom to find her plastered against a similar window with basically the same view I'd just been staring at, but Elaina's was over a giant bathtub I hoped we got to enjoy together at some point.

Stepping up from behind, I wrapped my arms around her and rested my chin on the top of her head. "Beautiful," I said, inhaling the scent of her that had become my addiction.

"I know, it really is," she said, bringing her hands up to tuck over where my arms intersected. I loved whenever Elaina touched me. And I soaked up every single touch she offered no matter how small or how fleeting. The unique feel of her hands reaching out to touch me meant something. Knowing she gave to me so freely also meant something, and I would cherish the memories of our time together when we were separated. It would get me through the rough patches. I hoped. I got a flash feeling of panic at the thought of leaving her behind in England once my R & R was up. *Don't think about it.*

I turned her around and took her face in my hands. I held her to me, searching her questioning eyes and tracing over her beautiful features, memorizing every small detail of what made Elaina the most beautiful woman in the world to me.

"I wasn't talking about the view," I told her, before I took her mouth with mine.

I kissed her for a long time in front of that picture window. I cherished my girl until I was good and satisfied. Until I'd tasted her enough to let her go so I could make good on my promise to stare at her over dinner.

We were definitely a little late.

Elaina's blush at the server when he came to seat us, and the looks of the other guests, probably guessing the reason behind our tardiness to dinner, caused all kinds of protective urges in me. One look at Elaina, and anyone could see from her flushed complexion and puffy lips from all the kissing, and have pretty good idea about what we'd been up to.

I slid my hand possessively down to the small of her back and led her to her chair, seating her first, the way my gran had taught me. I wanted all those people to know she was mine. If I could've managed it without everyone believing I was a complete nutter, I would've made an announcement too. *This beautiful girl is mine, people, and she loves me.*

I figured either way, I came out winning, nutter or no. I still got to stare across the table at her over dinner.

9

"What do you like best about being a captain in the Special Forces? You don't talk much about it."

"We're not supposed to talk about it, darlin'."

Her face fell and her lips made an adorable pout that made me want to do things to them that required a locking door.

"Well, what can you tell me? I need to know something about what you do over there in Afghanistan."

I shrugged over my plate of perfectly cooked venison and gave her the most honest answer I could. "It's just work that's been a good opportunity for someone like me, I suppose. Hard work and very dreadful at times. Lonely.

Harsh. Dry. Fucked up." I looked up from my dinner into her caring eyes, and for the first time ever, wished I wasn't a soldier.

"Sounds wonderful," she said sarcastically. "How much do I need to worry about you coming back to me safely, Neil?"

I covered her hand with mine. "I'm coming back in ten months and when I do it'll be for good. That'll make a six-year haul for me, and it's plenty, believe me. I want to do something else with my life, and I promise this is my last tour, Elaina."

"Thank God." Her voice was relieved but the concern still showed in her face.

"It feels nice to have you worrying about me, though."

"I've always worried about you, I just wasn't privy to what was going on before. Now, it's different. Now, I'm bloody terrified that something bad will take you from me, that I'll lose you—that we'll never have our...time together."

"No." I shook my head. "I'm not accepting that. I'm going over there and I'll do my job, and when my time's up, I'm coming home to you. That's a promise I'm going to keep." I picked up her hand and held it against my mouth. "I love this hand so much."

Her eyes grew watery when I said the last part.

"I love the man holding my hand. So much," she

whispered with teary eyes, "and I want him to come back to me in one piece."

I knew it was time. Time for us to be close and put away all the doubts we'd both carried around for far too long. Time for us to learn what we had to lose by not being together, and making us both see how we couldn't live without it for another second.

"Look into my eyes when I tell you that I'm coming back. I will. I'll be gettin' off a plane and scanning the crowd for my Cherry Girl to come running up to me, where I can pick her up and hold her very close, and know we'll never have to be separated again."

She nodded imperceptibly, her eyes still glassy and beautifully blue in the candlelight across from me. "Promise?"

"With everything I've got in me."

I saw her visibly soften in her seat, the tension lessening some, and wished we were alone and not in a room with others. *It's time to take her upstairs and love her completely.*

I whispered so only she could hear. "I need to be with you now, and we can make all these worries and fears about all the bad things that frighten us, just disappear," I spoke with my lips up against her hand and my eyes on hers. "We can make it all go away, for tonight."

"Yes, please." A single tear slipped down her smooth cheek as she nodded her agreement at me from across the table.

I got my answer and it was all I needed.

We held hands all the way up to the room, passing by museum-worthy portraits, which were at least eight feet tall, mounted on the stairwell, and artwork of amazing forms and variety. I couldn't really take in what was around me, though. I only cared about the girl beside me.

Once the stairs were behind us, I swooped her up and carried her the rest of the way. I wanted her weight in my arms. I wanted to carry her to the place where we would be together.

"You're going to hurt your back by hefting me around."

"Not a chance of that happening, beautiful girl. You're a feather. My arms love the feel of carrying you, so I think you'd better get used to it."

My Cherry blushed for me, looking shy and mouthwatering, just by being her sweet self. "Put your arms around my neck," I said.

She complied with my request, her small hands sliding up around me to hold on firmly. It felt like heaven. I dropped a kiss on her while holding her up, somehow managing to get the door open and thankful for old fashioned doorknobs that weren't locked from the outside. I didn't want to let go of her mouth as I fumbled with doors and locks to get us situated inside, finally into some privacy. I needed the connection. I felt a growing desperation to complete us, like, if I waited another day it would be too late to claim her as mine, that somehow she would be lost to me.

I reluctantly set her down on her feet, steadying her until she found her legs. She looked up at me with hooded eyes, and kicked off her shoes.

I pushed mine off as well.

She bit down on one side of her lip in a way that made me so hard, I let out a groan. "You're so damn sexy when you do that."

She didn't respond except to start unbuttoning my shirt. Those perfect white teeth of hers biting down on her pink bottom lip, just about had me losing my business before we got started.

"I love sky blue. It's my favorite colour, you know." She finished the buttons and pushed my shirt off my shoulders the rest of the way. "It looks good on you, too."

"I love the way you take my shirts off me, and I'll be sure to wear this colour for you again."

"Your turn," she said, presenting her back to me.

I reached for the zipper on the back of her dress and took it down, sliding the silky straps off her arms. With nothing to hold it up, it dropped down to the floor the second I let go. She turned back around to face me in nothing but her knickers and bra. Sky-blue lace. Matching set.

Gods help me.

My eyes were still admiring, when I felt Elaina's

hands on my belt, and then the tug on the zip of my trousers. I kicked those bastards off so fast, that they flew across the room, the belt crashing into a table leg with a clank. Not much separating us then, just a few bits of cloth, and maybe a little temperance of being careful to do our first night right. The noise of my belt crashing notched up the passion a bit, and sort of gave the green light for everything we were about to do.

Worked just fine for me. I was desperate. I could go slow later and take my time making love to her all night. Oh, I would no doubt, but then…then I just needed to be as close as it was possible to be with her. I needed to feel Elaina naked—skin on skin with me, and that was pretty much it.

The two scraps of pale blue lace were all that she had on, and even that was too damn much. I wanted my fantasy vision from earlier. My Cherry Girl completely naked in front of the window.

My mouth found its way to her skin, anything I could reach—her neck, her throat, her shoulder, her ear, her mouth—as long as I was touching her, kissing her, all was fine.

Getting her bra unhooked was a challenge because my bloody fingers didn't want to cooperate, and I wasn't willing to destroy such a pretty garment, but if it came down to a battle between that lacy bra and me, then hell if I was going to be the loser. I tugged again, still with little success, when she stilled my hand and took a step backward. "Let me."

I watched as she reached her hands around behind

her back, and worked some magnificent magic. The
damn thing came unhooked.

Elaina stood and paused a moment before sliding
down one strap off her shoulder and down her arm.

I swallowed.

Then she took down the strap on the other shoulder.

My heart skipped a beat or two.

Sky-blue lace fell with a metallic click of the clasp
hitting the wooden floor.

*Oh fuckin' hell, she's more lovely than I ever imagined she
could be.*

Elaina was beautifully made, no doubt, but then this
was not news to me, either. I'd always known she'd be
perfect. I guess what blew me away was just how amazing
a thing it was for her to trust me enough, to offer herself
to me, to want me. That and the fact I was the lucky
bastard getting the offer, and the chance to see her like
this.

"You take my breath away, beautiful girl." I stepped
forward and palmed the weight of one perfectly sized
breast. She arched back with a soft cry when I touched
her nipple with my fingers and tugged gently to make it
pucker up.

"So do you," she whispered.

I dipped my head down to the other nipple and did
the same to it with my tongue instead of my fingers. I got

drunk on the taste and feel of her gorgeous tits in my mouth and hands.

I was greedy with her, alternating between the two until I couldn't wait to see my vision of her standing before the window another second.

No, I hadn't forgotten. My desperate fuckin' wish was going to happen or I'd die trying.

I dragged my mouth off one breast with a suctioned pull, her hands still buried in my hair, the angled arch of her body positioned to give me access, the sexy protest rolling out of her throat as I released her, all signals showing me she wanted this just as much as I did.

"Don't stop," she begged, tightening her grip to keep me close.

"I want to have you naked in front of the window," I blurted.

She stilled, loosening her hold, letting her hands fall down to my shoulders. Her beautiful blue eyes locked onto mine and I knew she was going to do it.

Slowly dragging those magic hands of hers over my shoulders, she raked them across my chest, tracing around each of my nipples with a finger before pulling away from me completely.

The cock-and-balls party in full force down below, was in violation of disturbing the peace, but I couldn't do a thing about it.

Elaina's hands came to rest on the only garment still covering her body. Those pale blue, skimpy lace knickers. *Just fuckin' kill me already before I die an inhumane death.*

She slipped her thumbs beneath lace at each hip.

That inhumane death I was worried about was going to happen regardless of my fears, and the meaning behind the expression "exquisite torture" made absolute perfect fuckin' sense to me too.

Just some simple life truths about Neil Emmett McManus. Accepted and understood.

My cock was agonizingly hard in my shorts, as time slowed down to imperceptible increments of forward movement. I'd waited so long for this, and wanted her so desperately, it was all I could manage to hold myself back—to control the urge to pull her beneath me and bury myself inside her—until the raging ache to claim her got some relief. I wanted to. I needed to.

I'd passed the point of no return with Elaina, and realized the signs clearly. No more waiting or enduring the agony of seeing her with other men, knowing they were getting something that was meant to belong only to me. I simply had to be connected to her, in both body and spirit, in order to soothe the savage craving tormenting me from the inside out for so long.

I forced myself to breathe deeply, watching as my beautiful girl slipped the lacy blue knickers over her hips, down those toned gorgeous legs of hers, gave a sexy little kick with a pointed foot, first with one leg and then the other, until the scrap landed silently somewhere in the room.

Fuck me into next week. I think I did die a bit watching her sexy strip show, my pathetic brain on such extreme sensual overload, there wasn't much more I could do except expire while I took in the sight of the perfect beauty before me. My eyes still worked, even if my mind had gone to Elaina Land and was stumbling around gleefully with no clear direction other than, *I have you naked in front of the window right now, and I'll be inside you even sooner.* She'd given me the most beautiful gift.

Her hair was luxuriously dark and silky, falling to midway down her back. I wanted to take it in handfuls to bind her against me while we fucked, using the length of it for leverage. I had so many ideas about what we could do, but, I could only breathe and stare.

I'd had a healthy obsession with her hair for years—this I knew. Hell, it was the basis for the nickname I'd bestowed on her when she was young, and right then, was serving as her only covering. The mahogany red waves flowing down her shoulders and trailing over one breast but leaving the other bare, made my fantasy vision, utterly complete in every way.

Wordless. There weren't any I could have used to describe her at that point. Useless to even try. She was beautiful, and naked, and wanting me to make love to her for the first time. Nothing else existed.

I prayed I would never forget how she looked to me in that moment, and I made a vow not to allow it to happen.

My body screamed with the need to kiss every

beautiful part of her, but that would take hours to do properly and I couldn't wait hours. Hell, I couldn't even wait seconds. That train had blown through town already with no waiting, no stopping, and no changing.

But, Elaina didn't seem like she wanted things to be any different.

Christ, she's so perfect...

I'm not sure how exactly, but I maneuvered us to the bed with Elaina laid out like a goddess upon it, my window fantasy but a distant memory, as I sat back on my knees and tried to decide where to *go* first. She had a body that took my breath away, and I planned on touching every bit of it, the need to know how she felt under my hands and mouth as necessary as breathing.

"What is it?" she asked.

"You're so fuckin' gorgeous I hardly know where to begin."

"Kiss me." She arched her whole body, offering herself up in the most beautiful way I lost the ability for coherent speech. The point was moot anyway, as my mouth got busy in ways other than talking.

I slid my hands over her slowly, beginning at her throat and moving down, learning her soft curves, feeling her reaction to my hands on her, listening to the sounds she made because of what I did with them.

When my mouth found its way to her breasts again, I slowed the pace, devoting some time to getting to know them intimately. I took the whole tip of one into my mouth and sucked, rolling the nipple with my tongue and grazing with my teeth. She cried out softly, arching toward me even more. Her beautiful tits were very sensitive apparently, and this was precisely the kind of knowledge I desired to know about my girl.

I focused my attentions onto her other breast, holding its soft weight in my hand while suckling with my mouth, nipping the hard-budded nipple gently with my teeth. I got some beautiful sounds out of her for that effort, and I made a mental note of it for the future. Sexy sounds of submission and the acceptance of my touch, allowing me to take what she was willingly giving to me.

I sucked and licked and worked my way around both of her breasts. I put so many love bites on her, that I couldn't count how many, when I finally stopped and looked over my handiwork. Just claiming what was mine.

And, I wasn't a bit sorry about marring the perfectness of her skin either. The marks I'd made with my mouth were symbols of what she meant to me, a tangible display of what we'd shared, and for our eyes only, to remember what we'd done on our first time together.

I needed so much more than that from her though.

My hand moved lower to skim over her flat belly. I heard the soft intake of breath, and felt a jerk when I covered her lips with mine at the same time my hand delved between her legs. My fingers touched perfection—felt how soft she was there, how wet, how ready for me.

"Ohhh, Neil," she moaned under my lips, "I want—
I need—I—please—"

She sounded blissfully frustrated and I loved it
because I was the one causing her to be that way. And, I
held the power to fix it for her too. Bloody perfect
position for me to be in, as well.

"I know, beautiful," I interrupted, "but you're gonna
come for me first."

I plied her folds with a finger, circling the slippery
nub of her clit until she was writhing underneath me,
crying out my name again and again, spilling tears onto
the bed sheets in passionate submission as she arched up
and convulsed. I watched her come apart, lost in her
response both physically and emotionally, thinking that I
could watch her orgasm over and over and it would never
be enough; I'd still want to give her more pleasure. Elaina
owned me completely and it was so good belonging to
someone. *So fuckin' good.* I belonged to her as much as
she belonged to me. Even more, really.

"I want you n-n-now," she panted on a whisper.

I knew what she was asking of me, and I was so
ready to give her what she wanted that I wasted no time in
reaching for the pack of condoms resting on the bedside
table and slid off my shorts.

Elaina was then the one watching the show.

As her eyes settled on my rock-hard cock, I
wondered if she was worried about how we'd fit. I'd have
to be careful with her, because I'd be wrecked if I ever
hurt her when we fucked. Not her. Not my Elaina. I felt

a rise of panic and realized I was close to losing it—the utter mindfuck I was experiencing over the real fucking we were about to do.

Pull yourself together.

She saw me put the condom packet between my teeth to open it.

"You don't really need that," she said, with a shake of her head.

"Yes, I do," I said, as I rolled it down the length of my cock. She might say we didn't need condoms, but I knew we did. Elaina meant far too much for me to take a risk on getting her pregnant when I was leaving so soon. What if we made a baby and I got myself blown up and she was left alone. No. Never. Elaina was too young for babies, anyway. Later…much later, we would get to that point. Marriage. Children. Yes, but later.

"Neil?" She tugged at my hips with her hands, begging.

"Yes," I said, soothing her quietly.

I settled above her, moving those long sexy legs of hers wide apart with my hands. I hovered with my lips, wanting my mouth on her pussy, and my tongue dipping inside for a first taste, but realized this wasn't the moment. We were both far too impatient.

Later I'd be doing it though, I vowed.

Elaina looked so beautiful spread underneath me I

knew I'd always remember the first time. The way she was offering herself. How she was willing to let me take the lead. I couldn't mess this up with her or I'd never forgive myself.

She smiled up at me, glassy eyed and mysterious. I felt movement over my stomach and then the touch of her small hand gripping my cock.

I hissed when she touched me, her lips slightly parted, breasts heaving from the heavy breathing, the anticipation…and felt her guide the head of my cock straight up against her quim.

Fuckin' hell, I was so lost.

We both jerked from the contact, that very first scorching hot intimate touch between us. But nearly inconsequential, because we were about to make that burn go even hotter—there would be explosions.

"I love you and want to be with you so badly," she said in a whisper.

Amazing. Elaina accepted my love for her. That fact alone was enough to bring me to my knees, but even greater was the knowledge that this beautiful girl wanted to be with *me*.

"I love you, Cherry." My answer came with a deep push of my cock inside her very wet heat where she accepted the whole hard length, arching her hips up to meet my thrust. Perfect fit. Everything about her was perfect. She moaned as I filled her up, soft and so fuckin' sexy, I lost my mind for a moment as I settled into her.

The grip of her pussy around my cock held me so tight, I worried I'd come far too soon for what I'd intended it to be. I hoped to make love to her all night, as many times as I could manage to get us there.

I brought my face close, framing her in with my hands and captive to my invasion of her body. I couldn't help it. I only knew this was the way it should be done. Take her and make it so good, she'd never want another man.

But it *was* good. We were *so* good.

"Is this all right?" I asked her.

She nodded back. "Love me."

"I do. I will. Always..."

Eye to eye and nose to nose I kept her looking at me as I began to move.

"You feel so good wrapped around me."

I thought I might die.

She moaned at me, the sweet sound of her like a cue to get down to it.

Her tight wet quim became my universe for the next minutes as we found our rhythm. I hoped it was the same for her with my cock, because that moment, right then...was life affirming and life changing. Making love with Elaina was a beautiful dance, and like nothing I'd ever experienced before with a woman. But then, any other times for me had not been with her… so never with anyone I loved. Comparisons were irrelevant anyway. And, again, pointless.

Waiting… I'd been waiting for it, and when it was happening, I felt more emotions coursing through me than I was used to dealing with. I hardly knew what I was doing besides getting lost inside her. She met me with every thrust, and drew back with every retreat. We were a perfect union of minds and bodies.

Every time I filled her up she made a soft little sound that wound me a little tighter with each stroke. "Oh, fuck, it's good with you, Cherry."

"Don't…s-top," she begged, throwing her head back onto the pillow.

"I won't." I moved faster and deeper and harder, more than happy to oblige my girl's request. I gripped her hips to steady us, the frenzy growing more abandoned with each second that passed, when I felt her start to convulse and shudder. A low breath came out of her throat as she jerked beneath me, her legs flexing tight around my thighs to keep me buried all the way inside her. She gripped my arms as she rode out her release.

Elaina's response was like a trigger, sending me off right behind her, my orgasm taking hold violently from somewhere deep, pumping out of me and into her like an explosion. Our eyes held onto each other as we stayed fused, the rush of pleasure still pulsing for both of us as we took in deep breaths of air, living in the moment.

She felt utterly soft, and looked so perfectly beautiful when I pulled out of her, that I couldn't bear to look away, and had to deal with disposing of the spent condom by feel.

"Stay with me," she demanded, with a tug on my arm.

As if I'd go anywhere.

"We're not even close to being done. That was just a warm up," I told her, before finding her lips and plunging my tongue inside her mouth. I kissed her long and deep, my need to be in her was barely fulfilled despite what had just happened.

She touched my face with her hand and traced down my cheek. "You loved me." The way in which she said it almost sounded sad to me, as if she was trying to come to grips with the idea of us. Maybe, it frightened her.

"I did." I pulled her hand on my face to my lips and kissed it. "Nothing could have stopped me from doing it, either," I said.

"Nothing?" she asked innocently.

"Nothing restricted to heaven and earth."

"You're sure about that are you?" She reached down and wrapped her hand around my now less than hard cock. My sweet girl liked to have a bit of fun teasing it seemed.

"I think someone needs a little demonstration of exactly how determined I am about loving you."

"Oh, I'm sure you'll be able to *eventually*." She laughed softly, her hand still gripping around my bare flesh, feeling divine as long as she was touching it.

"In a little while, Cherry, you'll get some more of that." I paused, waiting to drop my own teasing comeback on her. "But first...I'm gonna make *you* scream again."

"Ahhhh...Neil!" she gasped, when I shifted down the bed in a flash and spread her wide.

Her hips undulated against my hands holding her thighs open, sending my cock to attention despite the thorough workout mere moments before.

I was on a mission. To get to the place at the center of her that held me captivated. "With my mouth," I said, before descending on her pussy and staring at all the beauty right in front of me. She wasn't totally bare, but almost, the sexy strip of cherry-coloured hair making me crazed to have my mouth on her. *How blessed was I?*

Licking at her folds until they parted, I found her clit and circled over and over with my tongue, serving that little sweet spot with some extra special loving attentions. With Elaina at my mercy for the next minutes, I held her pinned open with my palms and feasted on her quim until I was satisfied with my results. She was shouting my name—as promised.

I kept her honest.

It took me a good while to reach that point though, because I was a very greedy bastard when it came to her. Tasting so fine, and so amazingly soft under my tongue—

my girl was nothing short of exquisite perfection. I took her over and over again like that…giving my cock some needed breaks for recovery in between all the fucking that happened along the way as well.

Nothing was done in small measures on our first night together. The sex went on for hours.

The best part was hearing the precious *I love you's* when I made her come. She did it every time, and I loved her even more for saying it. If that were even in the realm of possibility.

We didn't take our eyes or our hands off each other. Not the first time, and not any of the other times we made love that night. I was running out of days with my Cherry Girl, and I had to take every available second of time I could grab for us.

I begrudged even the moments when I had to close my eyes for sleep, and was only able to do so, because I could feel her against my skin.

And hear her steady breathing in the dark.

And smell the scent of her with every breath I took in.

10

I held onto her as night transformed into day—slowly caressing up and down her back while she slept—unwilling to break physical contact, in a pathetic attempt to keep everything status quo and my heart intact. I loved her so much.

But now, I had something precious to lose, and the stark knowledge of that fact terrified me down to my very bones.

So, we had finally found our way to this point together, bodies aligned, key to lock, lover to lover. Everything had felt as I'd always imagined it would feel, but then at the same time, it didn't, because there was no possible description of what we did together that first night, in a stately mansion, perched on the Somerset coast.

It'd been far more than a first shag session between two lovers. Far, far more.

I had waited so long for Elaina, I was nearly out of my rational mind at times, with all restraint just flying out the window in an instant. She'd put up with me throughout the whole night though, and never once stopped me in my raging need to have her. My beautiful girl really did love me, apparently. I didn't know how or why but I'd take it for the gift it was.

I opened my eyes at some point to her blue ones watching over me in silence. Her body was draped half on top of mine, leg thrown over, palm on my chest, our faces very close. "Wakey, wakey," she purred.

Her use of my same words the first time she woke up in bed with me, made me smile. She had a bit of tease in her and I loved that. "Ahh, the best waking I can ever remember actually. Can we do it like this every morning?"

She smiled and blushed, sending me into instant arousal, the need to take her yet again instinctual and primal. I kissed her instead.

She had to be pretty worn out by now. We'd done nothing but shag and sleep, with occasional breaks for the bathroom and hydration, all night long.

I pulled back from her mouth, caressing her face and tracing her lips with a finger. "How are you feeling today, beautiful girl?"

"Loved by you," she answered shyly.

Her simple answer and accompanying blush was enough to get me going and reaching for the box of condoms again.

"I can never do enough of that." I got myself wrapped, and my mouth sucking on her tits in record time.

Elaina arched and moaned for me, letting me know she wanted what I was doing, so I pulled her on top of me and snaked a hand between her legs. My immediate goal being to make sure she was primed and ready for me.

She was.

My beautiful girl was soaking wet and more than prepared for me to fuck her. Again. Maybe she was really fucking me. Either way, was all good, and we were ready to go.

I slipped my hands under her bum and lifted her over my cock. She helped to guide us on target and then dropped herself down, impaling herself hard on me.

"*Fuck*, yes!" I shouted, wondering if the poor people who lived here had been kept awake during night from all the noise. I know we made plenty.

I was so lost in my girl, my social filter was completely absent, and I didn't care if we were inconveniencing anybody. Just didn't care about anything or anyone but us.

She rode me expertly, lifting her hips again and again in a rotating motion that would see me utterly blown in a very short time. As soon as I made sure she was going off, I'd let myself follow. My Cherry came first. This was a rule. She. Came. First.

"Ahh…I'm coming…" she whispered, as she worked me over, her eyes starting to glaze as her whole body became overtaken by shudders.

Thank bloody hell.

I followed her within seconds, never taking my hands off her hips, slamming her down repeatedly onto my cock while I dissolved into her.

"I don't know what I think is more beautiful, this spread, or the view from our suite," she announced at breakfast.

We'd made our way out of the bed, miraculously, and down to the dining room. After our wake-up fuck, we'd showered together and even managed to get dressed into clothing fit for public wear. I think it really came down to the need for nutrients. Bodies can't shag for hours without some refueling to keep them going. The best kind of experiment though. I had no complaints as I sat across the breakfast table and watched her over a cup of tea and a scone. My only distracting thought—the long curl of hair strewn over her left breast, obstructing my view. My mind began playing the *let's remember what Elaina's tits look like naked* game. She had the most spectacular pair that's for sure.

Yeah, I'm just a lowly bastard male and cannot help

myself.

"What's on your mind, Neil?" She interrupted my inner ramblings.

I looked up to see her smirking and knew I was good and caught.

"Nothing fit for this fancy breakfast room full of guests."

"I knew it," she laughed.

"It's all your fault, my darlin'," I said. "I need to take you somewhere private and then I can show you exactly what was on my mind." I whispered the rest so nobody could hear. "After I remove some of your clothes."

"Ahh, I see what you're on about. You're trying to trick me back into bed with you and you should know that it's a lost cause, mister."

"Really?" I gave her a sad face.

She laughed at me some more, but said nothing.

"Well, it's a nice day today so maybe you fancy an out-of-doors shag?" I winked. "I'm game if you are, babe, I love me a bit country sunshine."

She shook her head at me and blushed beautifully. Man, did it wreak havoc on my insides. There was something about how Elaina got shy around me, and blushed at the mention of naughty deeds. That rosy flush of her skin that appeared when she thought about all the sexy things we'd done together, was definitely my kryptonite.

The day was perfectly fine and just about everything else was, too. Iridescent blue dragonflies flittered over the water, buzzing around us, and even occasionally coming to rest upon the water's surface. The fresh air mixed with the scent of her hair comforted my senses, to the point I could honestly admit I was blissed out. It was a first for me. I'd never known the feeling before.

Elaina lay back on my chest in a little green and white rowboat upon Lake Leticia, a scenic meandering pond situated on the Hallborough estate. I was again reminded of the many BBC miniseries my gran had enjoyed on TV when I was a boy—lovers from times past with nothing better to do than float on a garden lake, stealing kisses in their fine clothes and flattering their dates with fancy words.

I had to say it wasn't at all bad. I was loving it.

"My mum would love it here," she said, trailing a hand over the side and into the water. "She's always been captivated by historic homes and gardens."

"My gran would have, too." I surprised myself for mentioning her at all. Gran was a topic I kept close and pretty much closed. Elaina was different, of course, I could share with her, but it wasn't something I sought out to do. Thinking of my gran, I only wished I could have brought her to a place like this for a holiday. She would have loved the gardens and the ocean views, and the stately house very much. I never got the chance to take her anywhere nice or do anything special for—

"You lived with your grandmother before you came to England when you were seventeen?" she asked from the side of the boat, cutting off my retreat into past regrets I couldn't do anything to change.

"Yeah. In Glasgow."

"I knew that you were a Scot because Ian used to call you Scotty when you were younger."

"He changed his mind about it once I grew bigger than him, now didn't he?"

She laughed. "I remember that, too. Ian was so disappointed when you topped him in height."

"By like an inch, maybe. Your brother can be an idiot sometimes."

"Very true about Ian. But what happened to your mum?" She asked it softly, as if she were being gentle with me in case her question brought out sad feelings.

I rubbed up and down her arm to reassure her. "She had me when she was very young...just sixteen. My father was a student at the University of Glasgow when he met my mum and impregnated her. He abandoned us when she told him I was on the way. McManus was her family name, not his."

"So, you lived in Scotland with your mother and your grandmother?" She turned away from the water and asked me directly.

"Right. Her mother, my gran, took care of us, and then me, when Mum died. Yeah…it was pretty awful." Elaina pulled her hand from the water and leaned back against me again. She was waiting for me to talk about my past and I figured there was no time like the present. Hiding it certainly wouldn't help anything, and I might as well get on with throwing it all out there with her. I'd want to know if it was the other way 'round.

"When I was ten, my mother and her boyfriend got themselves killed in a car crash driving home drunk from the pub. They ran themselves off the road in a rainstorm and into a flooded ditch."

"Oh, that's horrible."

"Mum never really settled down like a typical mother. She had me far too young, and she didn't really grow up or get over the fact that my father didn't love her or want anything to do with us. She was only twenty-six when she died. And she had dreadful taste in men, apparently…" I trailed off with my sad story and hoped I didn't have to talk about it much more. I wanted to enjoy our time here, and not waste it on the uselessness of regret over things I had absolutely no control. Strolls down memory lane didn't do a bloody thing for me. I had learned to live in the present and for the future. It was the only way.

Elaina rolled over to face me and rested on my chest, looking up. "I didn't know all that about your family. I'm sorry."

"Sorry for what?"

"For you, for how scary it must have been for you as a little boy losing your mother and then later on, your grandmother. I knew it was bad for you, but I didn't know the story. I'm so sorry for your losses."

I shared more with her because she was so gentle and kind with her feelings, and I could tell she wanted to know about me. For the first time, I actually felt like talking a little about my life because I knew I could trust her.

"Gran was lovely...and if we're being completely honest, she's the one who really raised me. My mum was not ready to have a child and although my memories of her are sweet, we weren't ever like a typical mother and son. It was my gran's dying of cancer, when I was seventeen, that dealt the worst blow. It devastated me...and there was so little time to settle things before she passed away."

"You had to leave Scotland, then?" She found my hand and entwined our fingers together, caressing back and forth with her thumb.

"Yeah. And it was clear I'd have to go with my father as soon as Gran's condition was pronounced terminal. There was nobody else to take me."

She brought my hand to her lips and held it there.

I kept talking. "Everyone was unhappy about it. I didn't want to leave my home, or for my gran to die, or to go live with a father I'd never met, and who didn't want me any more than I wanted him."

She gripped my hand tighter.

"He had a wife who *really* didn't want me around—messing up their perfect little family life in England, bringing up questions, destroying the façade of respectability they'd earned. They had a three-year-old son already. Sam—their real son."

"So, you came to live with your father and that's when we met you?" she asked softly.

"Yeah, but I didn't make it easy for any of us. As soon as I was delivered to my father's house and got a good feeling for how things were going to be with my new *family*, I ran away, sneaking off almost immediately, hitching rides all the way back to Scotland. It took a while, but they found me trying to live in the back of my gran's garage. My dad sent me off directly to school in London after that mess so I didn't have to live with them, and since our last names were different, nobody connected us as father and son. I was just a kid dumped at school by people who liked to pretend I didn't exist."

Elaina was quiet for a bit, just holding my hand to her lips and absorbing everything I'd told her. When she finally spoke, her voice had a detached ring to it as if she were making a confession. "I always hated your family. I never met them but I hated them just the same for how uncaring they were of you."

God, I loved her. "I always sort of sensed that from you, Cherry. Just made me love you more though."

She wasn't done. "But then, I probably shouldn't

hate them, because if they hadn't been so awful we might never have met you. Ian wouldn't have befriended you and dragged you home to us." She leaned up to find my lips for a kiss.

I clung to her as if she were a lifeline. "Your family probably saved my life," I whispered, holding her face close.

"How did we do that?" I could see tears in her eyes and knew it hurt her to hear all this horrible shit. I hoped it was the last time I ever had to speak of it with her. Elaina was only part of the good things that had happened in my life. She was the light to all that darkness. I was relieved to realize that the sorry, sad rest of my past, just didn't matter to me anymore.

"By wanting me. You always wanted me, Cherry, and I don't know why you did, but I *do* know that it was the thing that saved me. You and your family saved me."

She nodded and let out a sob. "Always did...and always will." Her hand started moving, rubbing over the place where my heart beat and the blood was pumped, showing me the truth behind her lovely words.

"But, I don't want you to dwell on it. Please, for me, don't think about it anymore because it's over and just doesn't matter. I survived because of you, and more importantly, I have you now. You're mine." I smiled. "That's all I care about." I kissed her for a long time.

I held onto my Elaina. I held her up against my heart, in that little rowboat on the idyllic lake, at the splendid English estate that felt like something out of a Dickens novel, and knew pretty much what complete happiness felt like, for the first time in my adult life.

All the sad shit and the fucked-up past was well behind us, where it belonged. I figured we only had good in our future to look forward to together.

No words could do justice to what I'd just shared with Elaina in such a very special place. It was that meaningful to me. I certainly couldn't find the right words to express what it meant to me to know that she'd always loved me and wanted me...just because she did. No other reason, than that the path of her heart led her to me. A miracle. I couldn't rationalize it and I wouldn't even attempt to figure out why things played out the way that they did with us.

I made a decision to just believe in fate right then and there. Done. I wouldn't question the how's or the why's of it anymore, but simply accept the gift of fate I'd been given with my Elaina.

I'd hold the memory of this beautiful time together with her, keeping it safe inside me where I could revisit whenever I needed to, so I could make it through the next ten months of being apart.

And that time was coming.

Far, far too soon.

11

The enormous bathtub had a view to rival the best scenic vistas on any travel documentary, but I wasn't looking at or caring about it. No, my attention was elsewhere. And my view was much more spectacular.

Elaina, naked was breathtaking. Elaina, naked, and wet in the bath with me, even more so. Elaina, naked, wet, and sucking on my cock, was probably going to render me blind in the next minute or two. If I wasn't dead by then.

She worked me over good, drawing the length deep and pulling back with a little twist of her hand on each stroke. I held her long hair back from her face and let her take me to heaven.

Cherry Girl

"Oh fuck, fuck, fuck…that's it—I'm going off!"

I tried to pull away but she wouldn't let go and the wet warmth of her mouth felt too good against the bare flesh of my cock. I couldn't stop the force of the spunk that exploded from me, and worried about choking her, but I was too far gone to do much of anything about it. My state of control over myself had come and gone. I'd come hard.

She took it all down her throat while I shuddered and pulsed, feeling like I shouldn't do that to her, but it felt too fuckin' good to stop. I was a slave to her love and very happy to my lot in life.

"God, girl, you're gonna kill me," I said, panting through the after-rush of my orgasm.

She released me from her lips and grinned like the devil, wiping the corner of her mouth with a finger.

I groaned from the sheer pornographic lust she instilled in me. In a very good way of course, but still… "Yeah, I'm dyin' for sure."

"Nope. No killing you off, Captain. No dying allowed, either." Her hand still gripping 'round my cock, she stroked me slowly, still managing to keep me hard, which was not really an issue, ever, with her. I wanted Elaina all the time, and she was so generous with me; I just took and took some more. If she wanted me, I was ready to serve which was just another reason to be careful with the extra protection. With all the spunk going off from all the sex, it would just be a matter of time until I knocked her up. I couldn't let that happen.

"I love you so much it scares me," I whispered. "Come here, beautiful girl." I pulled her up my body to lie on my chest, her breasts pressing against me, her cheek just below my shoulder. I trailed fingers through her hair and just held her. How in the hell was I going to survive ten months without her? I really couldn't bear to think about it at that point.

This was one fact I did understand. Denial worked pretty well for me at times.

"I've loved you for so long a time it makes me afraid this is all a dream," she said. "I'm so afraid of losing all of this with you, Neil."

"No. You're not losing me. I'm here right now, and when I'm gone away I'll still be with you every day inside here," I said, placing a hand over her heart, "until we're together again, and I can have my hands on you."

She snuggled closer and held me a little tighter.

"Do you believe me?" I asked carefully.

I felt her nod into my shoulder but she stayed quiet.

"What's wrong? Just afraid?"

"Yeah."

Something was on her mind I could tell.

"Are you going to tell me what's bothering you, Cherry, because I need to know."

She traced her fingertip over one of my nipples, making a shiver roll through me, and sending my cock on the fast track to recovery.

"It's nothing...I'm just selfish with you. I want you all to myself and I never want to share you with anybody." She looked up at me. "I want it all. You need to know that I won't share you, Neil. I can't do it and I won't." Her voice was harder than usual and the meaning behind the tone worried me a little.

"What do you mean? Share me with...other girls?" I shook my head. "There's nobody but you. Elaina? What is all this about?"

She shook her head again.

I gripped her a little tighter. "Tell me, darlin', what has you worried about me?"

She swallowed and looked down. "Well, you're— you are always so careful with us when we have sex. Always so careful about the condoms...and you don't need to be that way. I've told you I'm on the pill and it bothers me that you—that you don't want to be all the way close with me...like you're afraid to make the commitment, or—or s-something with me."

Silence.

I learned a valuable lesson in that moment. Never, ever, *ever*, assume you know what a woman is thinking in her head. That way leads to utter confusion and disaster. Elaina had read me all sorts of ways of wrong.

"Oh, Cherry, you want to know why I am so careful about wrapping up every time?"

"Yes." She nodded with a sad look in her beautiful blue eyes.

"It's not because I'm thinking of who next I might bang, because there's nobody. I'm only thinking of you." I kissed the top of her head. "Of how much I love you." Another kiss. "Of how precious you are, and how determined I am to make our life perfect together." I lifted her face up. "There's nobody else I'm committed to, Cherry. Only you. I'm not going to fuck it up by getting you pregnant before I go off to war. That would hurt *you*. No unplanned babies for us. I won't do that to you, and I won't do it to an innocent child. I was one of those babies and I absolutely won't do it to one of mine. What if something happened to me over there and I couldn't come home to you? If you were left alone to raise a child without me. You're too young for all that and it's irresponsible of me to risk that. I will never risk *you*, Elaina. I love you too much."

Her face cupped in my hands, she nodded up at me. "But I would want anything that came from you, from us loving each other. No baby of yours could ever be unwanted by me, Neil. Surely you know that."

God, she was amazing. "I do now." I smiled at her. "And some day we will make a few together, and they will be so beautiful with you for a mum."

"With you for a dad," she said with a gorgeous smile.

"Feeling better now that we've planned out our future together?" I asked.

"Yes." She shifted in the water and brought her lips down to kiss my chest right over my heart.

The gesture did something to me. Elaina was my switch. Or more so, she was the person who operated my switch. She controlled me, and I was perfectly happy with that arrangement.

As her lips trailed over my chest and even lower for parts desperate to feel her touch again, I was lost. Lost and desperate to find my way back inside her. Driven to claim her body more times than I needed to, but she felt so good, I couldn't stop myself from doing it.

So, that's what I did for the rest of the morning…focused on my girl and making her come so many times, she just had to forget about the worries and fears that bothered her. She had me to carry that burden for her. I'd make sure my Cherry Girl never had to worry about anything. I'd always be there for her, loving her and taking care of her.

I fully intended to. My motives were sound, but my naiveté completely shrouded the twisting paths of fate and how it can rear up and take everything away from you in an instant. One should never underestimate what fate has in store for you. It has a way of gaining the upper hand and can hold onto that power for a long, long time.

I *was* that naive.

"Hold still, this is a great shot of you." Taking pictures of Elaina was becoming my new favorite pastime. She was a magnificent subject anyway. The particular shot of her, under a flowering tree loaded with pale pink blossoms, was so perfect for her. We thought it was some kind of ornamental cherry tree from how the flowers looked. My Cherry Girl under a cherry tree. Cliché yes, but spectacular all the same, and I fully intended to have some prints made that I could frame.

"The blossoms are everywhere. It's almost like snow." She spun around with her arms out.

I took photo after photo while she indulged me, so grateful I'd have this beautiful memory of us there together on the last day before we had to head back home.

"So what do you want to do on our last day, beautiful girl?"

She made a face at me and circled around the tree trunk. "Oh, I haven't told you my news yet."

I lowered my camera. "What news?"

She peeked around the tree at me. "The news about how I'm not going back to London at all. I'll be staying here under this cherry tree, and taking boat rides on Lake Leticia every day, and watching the dragonflies flitting over the water."

I made my way over to her. "Really."

She moved around to the other side of the tree. "Yes, really. I thought you should be aware of it since you're going to be living here with me." Her expression was deadpan.

I started to reach for her but she moved again, switching to the other side of the tree trunk. My sweetheart liked a bit of fun and games at times. "You want me to stay here with you under this cherry tree, Cherry?" I asked slowly, my eyes tracking, picking my opportunity to lunge for her.

She nodded and shifted again to the other side, keeping me at a distance, her eyes tracking me, just as much and I was her. "You have to stay here with me, Neil."

"I do, eh? Because you love me so much?" I inched closer.

Her expression betrayed her because she couldn't help the devilish gleam that appeared in her eyes when she shook her head. "No, I need someone to row the boat!"

I sprinted for her and she took off shrieking, both of us laughing when I got my hands on her, and pulled us down into the soft grass.

I trapped her beneath me and tickled first, getting lots of playful groping in between the kisses and general horseplay. She got some good digs in too, and damn if she discovered I was ticklish as hell in the ribs.

"Now, be a good girl and let me kiss you," I warned,

pinning her hands down to the grass so she couldn't get at me with more tickling.

Her eyes flared and she tilted her head to the side a bit, her hair strewn out around the grass with a few blossoms already fallen down to land all around us.

The softness in her expression, and the way her body melted into mine, I adored. She let me soak her up, and kiss her until we were both breathless, and wishing that time would just stop altogether.

We made out cloud shapes from the grassy bank with the cherry tree blossoms still floating down. By that time, we were covered in them, but it was futile to brush them away as more just kept falling. Neither of us seemed to mind and the blooms had just the barest light scent so they weren't overpowering at all.

"I see a leaping frog at two o'clock just there." I pointed. "See how his back legs are out and the webbed feet—"

"Oh look, Neil, don't move!"

I froze. We both stared at my outstretched finger where one of those glowing blue dragonflies had chosen to land. I brought my hand closer very slowly, and miraculously it stayed on my finger.

"It's so pretty. Just look at the colours of blue," she said softly, as we both studied the insect. Seemingly unperturbed by our presence, the dragonfly extended its wings and lifted its legs to take a step or two.

"Amazing that the colour is from nature isn't it?"

"It really is. Like a sky blue crossed with a metallic blue. I love it so much."

"You said that sky blue is your favorite colour." I felt the vibration of movement and then the dragonfly was off my finger and flying away.

"Oh, there he goes," she said, "and yeah, sky blue is my favorite." If I wasn't mistaken I'd say there was some sadness to her comment.

"Why do you love the colour of sky blue so much?"

"It's the colour of the sky when it's beautiful on a sunny day."

I nodded and looked back up at the sky, searching for more shapes.

"September 11 was a sunny day," she said very softly.

I understood my girl so well. She had reasons for most of the things she did, and this was a very good example of that.

"The colour of the sky reminds you of your dad."

She snuggled into my side. "Yeah. It's so pretty and soft looking. I like to think of him up there in the clouds of heaven or something. It was the last place I know where he was alive and it was such a beautiful day…" Her voice trailed off.

I toyed with her splayed-out hair as we lay on our backs, content to touch its silkiness, until I heard a soft sound, and felt a small shudder, as she turned and wept in the crook of my neck. Telling me had brought out very painful emotions. I understood how that worked. You were okay holding onto your deepest feelings just fine, but as soon as you shared them with somebody, the flood of hurt came busting out.

"He's there waiting for you, Cherry. He's proud of you and happy if you're happy. There's no pain or sadness where your dad is."

"How do you know?" she asked.

"I just do. I have to believe in something and I believe in that. For your dad and my gran—the good people—they are in a better place now. And we can miss them, but I know they would only want us to be happy."

"I just love you so much," she told me, her eyes still brimming with tears.

"I love you so much, and I'll be coming home to you when I'm done with the army and we can start our life together. We've got nothing but time."

"Okay then, I'll be here waiting for you, right here at this cherry tree." She tried to give me a smile with her little tease, but I could see it was still hard for her. The next months would be hard on both of us.

"I know. When I return, we'll come back up here

for our reunion weekend." I pulled up her chin toward me and met her beautiful, sad face. "What do you say to that idea, darlin'? Back here at Hallborough, you and me, cherry blossoms, row boats and blue dragonflies."

"Better make it a week, Captain. A measly weekend just won't do for me."

"Thank the blessed gods for that, because I'm going to need lots and lots of long baths in that tub together before I'm even close to recovered from being separated from you, Cherry."

I held her close up against me and worried. I couldn't shake the feeling of gloom that hung in the air and feared I might be losing my mind. I tried to remember, that as I left for my tour that time, I was leaving England with the girl I *loved* waiting for me back home.

Elaina would wait for me. She'd needed the reassurance that I would always be her man, but we'd worked that out. I'd promised her there was nobody else who could take my heart away from her and I meant it with everything I had in me.

I closed my eyes and held her and prayed. I prayed that everything would play out, and fate would be kind, and my beautiful girl would be here for me when I came home.

12

Four weeks later

I woke with the weight of dread pressing in on me. I'd be returning to active duty in the morning so the day was our last one together, for more than ten long months of separation. The SAS might have me on a plane bound for Afghanistan within a day, but my heart would stay behind in London with Elaina.

The last twenty-four hours had been a marathon of emotional highs and lows and…sex, my need to claim her again and again, a compulsion that I couldn't hold back and couldn't bear to deny.

"How am I going to say goodbye to you at the station in the morning?" she asked in a soft voice, her hand brushing over my chest back and forth.

"I have no idea on this earth how I'll walk away from you. I just know that if you don't help me out by being strong, then the SAS will have an A.W.O.L. situation on their hands."

"That sounds very bad." She moved her hand up to my mouth where she traced my lips with her finger.

"Absent Without Leave *is* very bad."

"I finally got a letter from the International Placements office yesterday. I'd been waiting on it for a while, and there's a place for me in Italy. I was setting up to go away as an *au pair* before you came home on leave. You know about how I've been taking Italian and French in school, right? Well, I've been taking the courses so I could actually speak to my host family when I got a placement—"

"No. I don't want you to go." I moved over her and held her face. "Please promise me you won't go to Italy."

"Why, Neil? It's just a job." Her eyes searched mine. "And I'll be busy while you're away, and that'll help me pass the time. It's going to be dreadful here without you."

I could imagine some Italian count or wealthy playboy sweeping her away just as soon as he got a good look at her. "Ten months, my sweet beautiful girl. That's all I ask. I'll be home and we can go wherever you want then, but please wait for me. I—I just can't bear the idea of you not here waiting for me. I know it's a lot to ask, but I want you here where I know you're safe and with your family if something…happens."

"*Nothing* is going to happen," she said firmly. "Everything is going to be perfectly fine, Neil." Then her blue eyes softened and she smiled at me. "Okay, I won't go to Italy if it's so important to you. I'll find a job somewhere in the city. There must be a corporation that needs French and Italian because of international business."

"Thank you." I breathed out in relief before kissing my way down her body, pulling the sheet away with my teeth. The sheet peeled off, revealing her beautiful form in all its bare-skin glory.

"I need a picture of you like this to take with me," I blurted.

Her eyes widened but then she relaxed, as if she thought about it and decided I wasn't being a pathetic skeeve, but just a desperate bloke in love who was trying to hold onto her through any means possible.

"All right then," she said shyly. "You can take pictures of me."

So, I snapped some naked photos of my beautiful girl and would take them off to war with me. The pictures would help me to remember how sexy-beautiful and generous she was, how she smiled and how she spoke, how she smelled like flowers and looked like a Greek goddess, when I was alone at night with only my memories…and my hand.

Elaina had stepped out to the shops to buy our dinner while I packed up my things. She would keep my flat organized for me and also had use of my car while I was away. I loved the idea of her being here in my place even if I wasn't going to be here with her. It would help me to know we were together even when we weren't.

The doorbell rang and I wondered who it could possibly be. My goodbyes had been said to anyone who mattered. My father knew I was going and had sent his regards in an email. Typical. We conversed via written text, never on telephone, and rarely in person. He usually commanded my presence to his house if he felt the desire to see me. I didn't feel welcome in his home, so we were good.

Ian and his mum had already done a big send-off dinner for me, and I'd had the talk with him about Elaina, and how he needed to look out for her in my absence. And most importantly, keep that cocksucker, Tompkins away from her. My mates had been by to wish me off, promising pints in the pub upon my safe return.

I opened my door to find Cora standing on the other side of it and was really glad that Elaina had gone out. Seeing Cora at my flat would not make her happy. Not at all. Elaina really despised Cora and had made her feelings known from the very beginning that she was *persona non grata*. I got it. Tompkins was the same for me with her.

"What can I do for you, Cora?"

She smirked. "Where's your baby girlfriend, Neil?"

"None of your business, and her name is Elaina, as you well know." I wouldn't even address her other comment with a response. Pointless. "Look, I'm very busy getting ready to take off, so what is it that you want?"

"Only what you owe me, legally."

I'm sure my eyes popped out of my skull. "What in the hell are you talking about, woman. I don't owe you anything, legal or not."

Just at that moment, Elaina came up the stairs laden with shopping bags and smack into our conversation. Cora turned and said, "Oh good, she's here. You really need to know this too, doll." Cora fished out a small square paper from her purse and shoved it at me.

I looked at it. Felt my heart get ripped from my chest and then thrown down onto the floor so it could be kicked around like a football. "What the fuckin' hell is this, Cora?"

"That," she said with dramatic emphasis, "is our baby, Neil. Eight weeks gone. Isn't he cute?"

I looked at Elaina standing in the hallway, a shopping bag in each hand, just standing frozen in place, hearing every poisonous word. Her face was white as a sheet.

"No! No, Cora, no fuckin' way that's mine! Elaina?" I found her with my eyes and begged, "Cherry, *please* don't go away without—"

Cora ignored us both and kept right on blabbing. "Oh, but there *is* a way, darling. Eight weeks ago? Remember? You'd just come home from your long, long, lonely tour and were quite out of your mind as I recall. So many months without a woman...you needed a little something to take the edge off?" She snickered. "Quite a few times, too. Condom problems...it happens."

"No..." My gut churned, and the fear boiled over as her devastating words crushed my whole world. I had fucked Cora. More than once. The day I got home, I went straight to the pub and started drinking. By the time Cora showed up there, I was pissing drunk and horny enough to shag a troll. And we ended up at her place in a sex marathon that was all about gettin' off and nothing about feelings. I'd told her before we fucked that we weren't going to be together afterward. One of the condoms did blow out... Cora had said not to worry... *Oh. Fuck. No.*

I stared at the image on the black and white photo she'd handed to me.

It couldn't be mine. Could it? What would this do to Elaina? *FUCK!*

Cora turned and shrugged in Elaina's direction while I kept staring at what I held in my hand. "Well, that's all I wanted to tell you, darling. I know you're off in the morning and thought you should know that you're going to be a daddy. So take care of yourself over there. Be safe and all that rubbish, oh, and send me a cheque now and again. I have to pay the bills, you know, so I can take care of *your* child, Neil."

And then, Cora walked out as I stared at the doctor's scan and felt I might be sick. I didn't even say anything. I couldn't. I don't know how many moments passed. Could have been a few seconds, could have been an hour, but when I looked up, Elaina was gone. The only evidence to show she'd really been present to hear Cora's claim, were the two shopping bags full of our dinner sitting on the floor at the top of the stairs.

The hours that followed were something out of a horror film. I couldn't find her and I didn't know where she had gone off to. She wouldn't answer my calls or take my messages. Elaina's mum said she'd called to say I'd left a day early and she was going to stay with a school friend. Elaina didn't say which friend. Ian hadn't heard from her. Both her mother and brother were mystified as to what was going on and couldn't help me.

And I was out of time with no good options.

Desperate and terrified, I pulled every trick in the book trying to get an emergency extension of my tour, but was soundly vetoed. My final orders stood. Report to my commanding officer by the prescribed time in the morning, or be arrested and tried in military court.

That night was one of the longest, most horrible experiences I can remember. I didn't sleep for fear she might show up or ring me. She didn't, though.

The next morning I dragged myself to the train station in misery because my time was up. I scanned the platforms for any sign of her, my heart in shreds, terrified of what I'd say to her but desperately wishing for a chance to try to tell her how sorry I was, and how we could figure out what to do. I loved her, and couldn't lose her, and I'd make things work out—somehow.

My Cherry Girl wasn't there.

13

One year later

My final tour in the army had been the worst of my career. I saw the most dangerous action. The riskiest maneuvers attempted, some the closest I ever came to dying. The most loss of life experienced of troops I knew and commanded. Just a total fuckin' mess of events and situations all coalescing into a very dark time for me.

Coming out of it, I was a changed man. For many reasons, but the worst part was finally making it back home to London and finding out she really had gone. Elaina did take the *au pair* position and moved away to Italy to work within a few months of my leaving.

I'd lost my girl. My Cherry Girl was lost to me and I

faced the prospect of living a life without her. During my tour, she never contacted me once. Her mum and Ian still did, but kept out of our business and accepted that whatever had happened between us was not up for discussion, ensuring our privacy was respected. It felt like she'd died, she was that lost to me. I think it would have hurt less if she had died.

When I returned to my flat I found a letter from her dated the day I'd left for Afghanistan.

Dear Neil,

This is terribly hard for me to say, but I have to. I release you. You're free of anything you ever promised to me about us. I understand your situation and accept what you have to do about it. But, in order for me to survive it, I have to let you go. It's the only way I can manage to get on with my life, and I ask for you to do the same with me. Let me go. Don't come for me or try to change my mind. This is how it has to be now.

Goodbye, Neil, and please know that I'll be wishing for you great success in all that you do, and praying for your safe return home wherever and whenever that may be.

Be well,
Elaina

I read and reread her letter a hundred times. There were some water splotches on it and I imagined they could have been from her tears. I couldn't bear to throw it away, but there were many times I nearly did. The dark times when I was so very angry with her for not giving me a chance to tell her anything about what really happened.

No, I didn't get that from her. I didn't get the chance to tell her about what I'd been through in the war. I didn't get the chance to tell her of the new job opportunity I was offered from a fellow officer—who barely made it out of the army still breathing—a job we were determined to make into a success.

I didn't get to tell her about the bizarre turn of events that left me the sole inheritor of a Scottish estate belonging to a great uncle I'd never met. There was a house and land involved, along with a fair chunk of money, that left me in a very good place financially for the first time in my life. After actually seeing the place, I didn't get the opportunity to tell her about it, or say how much I knew she'd love the grounds, or the little lake, or the old cherry trees that blossomed on the property, reminding me so much of our trip to Hallborough.

Everything was fucked up and my heart was broken.

And, most importantly, I couldn't tell Elaina that I was definitely not the father of Cora's baby. I'd been willing to face up to the responsibility of providing for the child if it was mine of course, but it wasn't mine and Cora shared that with me as soon as her son was born. Whether she was being a decent human being or because it was instantly apparent I couldn't have fathered him, I don't know. The point was moot anyway, my loss too great to repair by then.

Cora had up and married the real father before I'd even returned home from my tour. A big Black bloke named Nigel. This was all confirmed when I saw them in the supermarket one day shortly after I got back. The little baby with all the chocolate skin belonged to somebody else. Cute though. I managed a very hollow-sounding "congratulations" and walked out of there, the bitter taste of injustice and anger fueling me forward.

I still desperately longed for Elaina, but the resentment burning inside me at her leaving without a word, had hardened me. So hard, that I closed off my emotions and accepted my fate. I'd known bitter disappointment and grief before and I'd lived through it. I was used to accepting things that hurt me terribly and crushed my heart. This was just another one of those.

I threw myself into work at Blackstone Security International, Ltd. as Vice President and Chief of Operations. The boss's number one. We offered security services to high-profile clientele, politicians, dignitaries, celebrities and even members of the Royal Family on occasion. I traveled around a great deal, learning the business with Blackstone and working jobs that paid me very well, but left little time for socializing. Didn't matter. I didn't want society anyway. Any desire I'd ever had for love was in the hands of one unique person and she didn't want *me* anymore.

I reached out to Elaina's mum and asked about her. She told me Elaina was happy at her job in Italy and that she'd requested I not try to contact her. She just wanted the freedom to live her life and held no ill will toward me for whatever had gone wrong with us, but I wasn't buying it. Of course she had ill will. She felt betrayed that I'd been with Cora. And then, I'd had to abandon her for the better part of a year with a horrible fuckin' break-up between us. The whole situation was worse than fucked up.

I stayed close with Elaina's mum and Ian, hoping for an opportunity where I might see her again, maybe on one of her visits home or something. That maybe, we'd get a chance to talk about what had happened with us. That maybe, seeing each other again would spark something and we could find our way back to that beautiful place where we'd been so in love.

I even grew desperate enough to track her down in Italy once, when I was there working on a job.

The Italian seaside in summer is a stunning place. The lush beauty seemed fitting somehow as the place where she was now living and working. Elaina deserved to have all that natural beauty surrounding her. That part made perfect sense to me.

I saw her from a distance on the beach in a sky-blue bikini and a floppy black hat. Even from far away I recognized her. How could I ever forget? She looked so beautiful, my eyes stung as I soaked her in. Long cherry-coloured hair blew in the wind and whipped down her back. Lovely legs that went on for miles took small steps in the thick sand in order to accommodate the little ones she brought with her.

Elaina had two small charges, both girls that looked to be close in age, one in each hand, and a big straw bag on her shoulder with their supplies for the day. It took everything in me not to rush up and take the bag away so I could carry it for her.

It fucking hurt to stay hidden, lurking in the shadows while she settled all three of them onto the beach. But stay hidden I did. In total agony.

I watched her build sandcastles with the girls until

the tide came in and washed over their creations.

Washed away...wiped clean...erased...gone... As if it had never been.

I couldn't bear to see anymore, and quickly realized it was not a good idea for me to be there stalking her. I felt ashamed for my covert methods and worse than if I'd never seen her again. Seeing Elaina once more with my eyes just made everything so much harder for me. I knew what I had to do.

The time had come for me to finally let her go.

Just as I was taking my last drink of her, she turned in my direction. Elaina turned to me and looked over. She couldn't see me, I knew because I was well hidden, but she felt me. I know she felt my presence.

I'll never stop loving you, Cherry Girl. Never. I can't stop...and I won't.

In that moment my heart just exploded, and what was left turned into a hardened mass of bits and pieces that weren't worth very much.

My heart stayed hardened like that for a good while, too. It had to in order for me to take my next breath and to function. So I learned to live with myself and got on with it. I didn't have much of a choice, and in the end, accepting the hand I'd been dealt was easier than bluffing over the shit cards I was holding.

I worked hard, and lived hard, doing those things that a man needs to do to survive, no matter how hollow the aftermath leaves you feeling.

I did the most difficult thing I'd ever had to do in all my life.

I let her go.

I let my Cherry Girl go.

PART THREE

And now these three remain:
faith, hope and love. But the greatest of these is love.

I Corinthians 13:13~

14

Five years later

Blackstone Security International, Ltd. was housed in a sleek high-rise building near the Liverpool Street station, in downtown London.

My new place of work.

The company did a great deal of global business and had need of a receptionist with some fluency in the languages of Europe. I had Italian and French down well enough—I was still working on the German and the Spanish.

As it turns out, this job was perfect for me in a lot of ways. I'd missed England in the nearly six years since I'd been gone, so it was lovely to be home again and close to my family. Three years in Italy, and two in France, had allowed me to experience other places and practice the native languages first hand. And since there would be opportunity for travel around Europe, the job at Blackstone Security was sort of a combination of both worlds for me, and I liked that.

When Mum suggested I apply for the position, I'd thought it was because a friend from her card club had suggested how well suited I was for the job. Frances Connery was executive assistant to the owner and a longtime friend of my mother's. My brother, Ian, had also put in a word for me apparently. He was a high-powered London solicitor now, and Blackstone Security International was one of his top clients. He worked in the same building, only two floors down, so we saw each other quite a bit. Sometimes a little too much, because I'd discovered just how much all the ladies loved Ian. And the reasons behind it. Disgusting hearing how good your brother was in bed. Bleh. Talk about someone who needed to settle down.

My new job seemed almost too good to be true, and I'd been only been working there for about two weeks, when I found out why.

"The team is back today from the job in Madrid. You'll get to meet Mr. Blackstone, finally. He'll probably be in later than usual though from all the traveling. I'll introduce you to him and the rest of the crew as soon as they all get in. Coffee, dear?" Frances, my immediate supervisor, gestured to the pot in the break room.

"Yes, please. I still have so many people to meet

before I know everyone that works here." Several were always out on large-scale team jobs, so the whole company was never all together at the same time.

"Not to worry, my dear."

She handed me a cup of coffee that I immediately started doctoring with sweetener.

"Well, I hope I'm a good fit for them, you know, Frances?"

"Oh, you are, dear, you are. You're doing an excellent job so far, and I know Ethan will be pleased to have someone with your skills here at BSI, now that there is so much international work for them."

"Thank you for that. I'm really loving it here. I'm nearly done with the contract from the Italian consulate and can get started on the others later today."

"You're a gem, darling," she said, breezing out of break room with her coffee.

I got back to work at my desk, engrossed in translation and fielding calls when the most handsome man came through reception. Handsome didn't really accurately describe him though, stunning was more like it. Dark hair, blue eyes, tall, built, serious, and acting like he owned the place. The light bulb went on. This was Ethan Blackstone, and he actually *did* own the place.

"Morning," he said, with a nod and a thorough look at me.

"Good morning, sir," I said as he passed. He used

his key code, and walked through to the main floor.

I blew out a breath and hoped I'd passed the boss's screening. This job really suited me and I wanted it to stick.

I preferred to take my lunch and eat outside in the courtyard if the weather was decent. If I had any extra time, I'd pull out my Kindle and read for a few minutes. I loved reading fiction of all kinds and found that if I purchased the popular books in other languages, it helped me stay sharp, and gave opportunity to master the ones I was still working on. I was enjoying JR Ward's *Lover Unbound* in Spanish and really captivated by the angst of urban vampires fighting extinction in the modern world. Until the space on the bench beside me was taken up, that is.

"Hello gorgeous, what have you brought for me today?" He poked a finger into my floral lunch bag and peered in.

"God, Denny, don't you ever stop?"

He took a grape from my bag and popped it into his mouth. "Why should I stop? You're back in England, and you work somewhere near, because you come out of that building over there like clockwork to eat your lunch." He nodded his head toward my building.

"Because I'm not interested?" I gave him a fake smile.

"Aww, baby, don't be harsh. I just want to take you out and show you a good time, you know, for old time's sake. What do you say?"

I set down my Kindle and gave him a patient look. "I say, dear Denny, for about the tenth time, no thank you." *Not for old time's sake, or new time's sake, or any future time's sake are we ever going out together.*

God, I could only imagine the scenario he'd have set up for "showing me a good time." No. Just no. I wasn't going back to an ex that had cheated on me with some slut in a back alley behind the pub.

Even though I wouldn't ever consider him, I had to say, Denny Tompkins surprised me in where he'd ended up. I'd have placed bets on prison. But according to him, he hadn't been to prison and was gainfully employed at his father's import business. I could only imagine what illicit goods they imported, but it was better than the street dealing I was pretty sure he used to do. Maybe, still did. Who knew? He'd been persistently stalking me on my lunch hours, since he'd spotted me down here in the courtyard on my second day of work.

"Are you finally going to tell me where you work today, baby?"

"Stop calling me 'baby' and no, I'm not. It's called an invasion of privacy, Denny, and you need to stop."

He smirked at me and tilted his head, his dark wavy hair falling over his eyebrows and making him look dreadfully charming. He might be a hooligan in a suit, but he was a very handsome man all the same.

"You're tough now, Elaina baby. What happened to the sweet young thing you used to be with me?" He put his hand on my leg. "We had good times together."

"She grew up. And watch how you talk to me. And stop groping me," I said firmly, while brushing his hand off my leg.

I remember how relentless he'd been with me after Neil left for Afghanistan, and before I went to Italy. I couldn't shake him then, either. Ian finally had to step in and make him stop pestering me to be with him again. He just wanted me back in his bed, but I wasn't interested. Denny had the persistence gene for sure, but was too dense to understand that no man would take Neil's place.

No, that spot was a permanently empty placement.

"All right, then. Until tomorrow, baby." He leaned in and gave me a peck on the cheek. He also reached into my lunch bag again and stole a few more grapes, before sauntering off.

I rolled my eyes and tried to get back into my book, wondering how in the hell, out of all the places in London, my new job put me smack dab in the same locale as my ex, Denny Tompkins. No luck had I, apparently.

With that thought, I gave up my decadent vampire book and gathered my things. I sought out the newsstand for some foreign papers instead. Reading the news in Italian or French kept me up to date with the foreign headlines, and sharp in a different way than just reading the language.

"That'll be two pound fifty." Muriel, the newsagent on the corner, was quite the character. She looked like something between a homeless crone and a Gypsy fortuneteller with her habit of attempting to predict the future. Her eyes were the most amazing greenish-hazel though, unlike any colour I'd ever seen. Just stunning.

"Here you go, Muriel, and keep it." I handed her a fiver.

"Ye be an angel ta me, so bless ye." She flashed me a horrific toothy grin. "Gimme your hand, girl. I'll read ye."

She took my right hand and held it at an angle. She traced over the lines of my palm with her gnarled finger and muttered as she named them. "Life, Health…Love." Her beautiful eyes snapped up to mine at the last one. "Ye have love comin' yer way, girl. True love is a comin' for ye." She smiled again.

Muriel's declaration rattled me. I pulled my hand out of her grasp, mumbled a quick "thanks" and left quickly with my newspapers, sure she was just trying to validate her fortuneteller act with me.

Seriously? True love was coming for me, huh? I wanted to laugh, but I didn't. The particular words she'd used were ridiculous, because I knew her prediction was totally false. I had only one true love, and I'd told him a long time ago…to never come for me.

I'd returned from lunch when Frances buzzed though and asked me to make my way down to the executive offices with the translations I'd done.

This was it. Meeting time. I tried to suppress the nerves suddenly making me jittery and prepared to leave my station.

I hurriedly gathered up my paperwork and folders and went to open the door using the security key code on the access panel. I punched in Z-A-R-A and got the door open successfully, but my paperwork not so much. The edge of the folder got jumbled on the door frame and I lost hold of it. The contents spilled out all over the floor at my feet.

"Well, shit."

I dropped down to pick up the pages, mortified and praying not too many people saw my blunder, when two well clad male feet stepped into my line of sight.

"Let me help you with that," he said, dropping down and beginning to pick up the mess of papers scattered at our feet.

"Thank you," I managed, too embarrassed to make eye contact when he handed a stack to me.

He rose up and so did I. Determined on organizing the pages in my now, very untidy folder, I was distracted and not paying close attention when I offered an introduction to my helper. "Sorry for that. I'm Elaina, the new reception—"

I drew my line of vision up a very large, suited chest, and met eyes I had looked into before. Dark, beautiful eyes, which had burned back at me with love in moments of deepest intimacy. Eyes I had loved…

I lost the rest of my words.

My heart hammered. Speechless didn't even begin to cover it. Breathless and dumbstruck needed to be in there too, because I dropped the folder again and heard the papers dump out in a heap at our feet with an airy swoosh.

"N-Neil."

"Elaina," he said stonily.

The hard frown on his face made him look as if he was just as surprised to see me, as I was to see him.

15

For fucks sake! *Elaina* was the new receptionist?!

My heart skipped and stuttered from inside my chest as I tried to process this bit of information. Frances had just mentioned to me, not a half hour ago, that we'd hired a new girl. Never in my wildest dreams...

Well, it all made sense to me now. I figured out who was behind it in an instant. And was going to kill the miserable sod just as soon as I could get my hands around his traitorous neck. Mum Morrison would get a pass on the strangling, but I was greatly annoyed with her, as well.

But first, I needed to look... Five years since my eyes had rested on her. Even longer than that, at a close enough distance to reach out and touch her. I dragged a hand along my scalp instead, gripping the back in a handful of hair and pulling hard until it stung.

Now *this* was a mindfuck in the purest sense. I was barely able to keep myself contained, my emotions and my body operating at odds and totally independent of one another. My Elaina—the woman I'd never stopped loving, the girl who'd captured my heart all those years ago, and who I'd painfully *let go*—was here before me claiming to be newly employed at BSI.

Fuck me into next week! And, then some more.

My thoughts were totally lost in a jumble of shock and disbelief.

Eons might have passed, I don't know, but yes, this was indeed a fuckin' blow to my sensibilities. I needed a drink, or a pitcher, or maybe I'd just sleep in the pub tonight. And I definitely felt a headache coming on.

"I—I didn't know..." she began. "Nobody said—I—I'm—ahh..."

I didn't register what she was saying because I couldn't. I just stared.

So, here she was again right in front of me. As beautiful as ever. More beautiful even than I remembered. No longer a girl of eighteen trying to find her way, but a woman of twenty-five with the confidence to go with the maturity.

Her confidence might be a tad lacking at that very moment, though. Those midnight-blue eyes reminded me of a deer caught in headlights. It took great effort on my part to keep from touching her. To reach out and embrace her was instinctual, and I wanted to, but I controlled the urge and waited for some kind of response from her. After all, she'd been the one to leave me hanging without letting me have my say. The wound from that gash to my heart was still there, freshly ripped open and dripping metaphorical blood down the front of me. I'd waited this long, I could wait some more.

"Wh—what are you doing here?" Her throat moved as she swallowed hard and made me want to put my mouth there and taste. I craved the experience of remembering the flavor of her skin, but more than anything, I wanted her to acknowledge *me* again. I wanted her to have to look at me, to talk to me, to accept me being near her. And, if I knew anything about Elaina, it was that she would try to flee from me again.

"I'm Chief of Operations here at BSI." I let that sink in for a moment and watched her beautiful complexion grow pale before my eyes.

"You work here." It was not a question, but a statement, as if she were trying to convince herself of this bit of news.

And I think I know just how you feel.

She pulled her hand through her hair and drew it down to rest in the hollow of her throat, like she was trying to protect herself. Interesting watching her terrified reaction to my bomb drop. Strangely, it made me happy at the same time. If she was instinctually seeking protection from my proximity then it meant that seeing me again was having some sort of effect on her. *Good.* If she was this affected by me just being there, then it had to be nothing compared to what I was experiencing in her presence. For so long, I'd wanted to be this close to Elaina again. *So long.* It almost felt surreal to finally get my wish after aching for it to happen. Years, I'd waited. I'd figured it would happen eventually because I was still close with her family, but I suppose I couldn't really have prepared myself for the actual reality. And, not like this. Working together in the same office? Jesus, God, and all the angels!

I felt numb.

I was indeed numb as I spoke my answer, not really quite sure how to break the news to her, when she was right in front of me.

"Every day since its founding, over five years ago." I nodded slowly, trying to keep it cool with her. "I served with E—Ethan, in the SF." I gestured with my hands up. "Yeah, all this was *waiting* for me when I came home from the war." *But you weren't, were you, Elaina?* I could be a bastard when I felt like it, and I have to say, I felt like it right then. Fuck, but I was entitled to something more than this stilted, chilly reunion. I'd known her since forever and we were reduced to this awkward silence and distance after where we'd been together? But, that was the problem wasn't it? The part where we'd been together. And all the intervening years when we hadn't.

The whole thing was pretty fucked up. But, I was used to that in my life, though. Lots and lots of fucked up had made its presence known to me over the years. I didn't remember a time when it hadn't, but Elaina was never part of all the bad in my life. She was the good. Only good...at least that's how I remembered it...until the very end. The ending of us had nearly destroyed me.

I hoped for some kind of reaction from her, something. Anything at all would do.

"Oh, okay…" Her eyes flickered over me for an instant and then down and to the side. This was all definitely a surprise for her, too. *Good. Again.*

I saw her breathing hitch, and remembered what she'd been like when I'd had her beneath me and about to come. Those sexy breaths of air as she'd shuddered around me. The tight grip of her pussy squeezing around my cock when I was inside her…

I couldn't help what I said to her next. "Looks like we're going to be workmates, Elaina."

"Ahh...yeah." She did something that I wasn't expecting then. She bit down on one side of her bottom lip and pulled it into her mouth a little, a look of discomfort flashing across her face as if experiencing pain. That's what it looked like at least, and I felt some kind of small victory. The comment about this job "waiting" for me was a dickhead move on my part, but it came out of my mouth and I wasn't calling it back. It was the truth even if it gave me no satisfaction. She moved to pass me in the space of the pathway. "Frances is expecting me in her office...we're going over some contracts I've just translated..."

"Would those be them?" I pointed to the floor.

"Shit." She dropped down again and started grabbing up the pages, the short black skirt she wore riding up quite nicely along her legs as she worked. She was clearly embarrassed and I could see the flush in the tops of her cheeks as they reddened.

My cock reacted the instant I saw the rosy blush appear in her skin. *Just like old times.*

I bent down to help once more and caught a whiff of her perfume, the scent taking me right back to six years ago as if only mere moments had passed. "Do you think you'll be able to get that file down the hall to Frances, or shall I escort you?"

Inhaling sharply at my comment, she snatched the last paper from my hand and shoved it sideways into the folder. "I should be able to make it this time, thank you," she said with a bite of sarcasm.

"Good luck, then," I said, standing up yet again and offering my hand to assist her. "Focus, Miss Morrison." I forced a smile.

Surprisingly, she accepted my hand and let me pull her back up. At least there was some contact. Hands. My hand was on hers and I didn't want to let go. I wanted to tug her against me and carry her off somewhere private. I wanted to demand to hear her story and I wanted to make her listen to mine. We deserved that much. Both of us deserved at least that little bit of honest communication for closure, if nothing else.

Elaina released my hand and attempted to tug her skirt down without losing the file for a third time. Quite the feat for her apparently, and I had my doubts about whether the file would make it safely to Frances's office or not.

I very much enjoyed watching her try though, just as I enjoyed the view of her magnificent arse from behind in that short skirt as she walked away.

My sweet Cherry Girl was back in my life whether she liked it or not. I knew where she lived and I knew where to expect her every day for work. I would get to see her and she would even have to talk to me. I was her superior here, and she didn't have a choice in that.

She might still hate me and never give me another chance with her, but we'd just have to see what happened, now wouldn't we?

I had a task that needed my attention, or rather a best mate that needed murdering.

I went straight out, left the forty-fourth floor and down to number forty-two. I sailed past Ian's secretary, holding my hand up to her surprised protest, and barged into his office.

He was speaking into the telephone but I ended his call for him. I stabbed the red button several times and disconnected him.

"What the fuck, Neil?" Ian glared at me. "I'm taking a call of business here. Do you mind?"

"Yes, I do in fact mind very much, you meddling cocksucker! What in the fuckin' hell are you on about bringing Elaina to work at BSI?"

Ian sat back in his leather desk chair and folded his

hands in his lap, looking smug and cocky. "My sister needed a job, and well, it's a perfect fit for her…in every way. Frances, Mum, everyone agrees." He flipped his dark blue eyes, which matched Elaina's to perfection, up to peg me hard. "Wouldn't you agree as well, mate?"

I pointed at him, my outstretched finger visibly shaking. "I would agree that you're a fuckin' arsehole, how's that for agreement?"

Ian shrugged, picking up the telephone and redialing. "Sticks and stones, brother."

"How about staying *out* of my business…*brother*." I was so angry at being played, I knew I had to leave before I committed a heinous assault on the bloke I considered my brother, even though by blood he wasn't. "Fuck off, Ian," I said, turning to go.

"You're welcome, Neil," Ian called out cheerfully, "we'll talk later at the pub."

If I don't kill you first.

16

I slammed into the house I'd grown up in and started yelling.

"Mum, how could you?" I demanded, throwing my purse down on the table and kicking off my heels. "You knew Neil worked at Blackstone Security, didn't you? You set me up, and Ian too, the bastard."

"Now, darling, please don't be upset, but think about your new job and how much you've loved working there in just the short time you've been employed. It's a marvelous opportunity for you. And I know you love Neil despite whatever happened between you two," she admonished.

Yeah, and this is not news to me, Mum. I glared at my

mother, totally unbelieving she'd done something so manipulative and underhanded to me.

"And he is so good to me…" she trailed off, taking a sip of her six o'clock gin and tonic while trying to look innocent. She was damn good at it, too.

"Did Neil suggest to you to get me to apply for the job? Did he ask Ian to recommend me?" Realization dawned and I felt the urge to thrash somebody. "Wait—what do you mean *Neil is always so good to you*, Mum?" I was absolutely fuming with the knowledge I'd been duped by my own family to bring me back to England, and to Neil. But something didn't ring true with my theory. Neil did not act like he was expecting me. In fact, he looked completely and utterly shocked at seeing me again. Nobody had told him I'd been hired, I would bet my bank account.

It all made sudden sense. My family was conspiring to get us back together.

Not. Going. To. Happen.

"Well, Neil's always been a lovely boy, Elaina darling. You know that about him. Such a help, especially after your father died." She took another healthy slug of her G&T and sniffed. "He—he checks in on me quite regularly, my dear, I just never said anything to you about him because he specifically asked us not to bother you with it."

"Is that so, Mum? Are you taking me for a walk later? Down a plank? Set out over the shark infested ocean?"

I was in shock at what they had done.

"Oh, don't be so melodramatic, Elaina."

"MUM." My mother really needed to take her own advice about the melodrama but she ignored me and kept right on singing Neil's praises.

"He took care of the service on my car and helped me when that horrible storm knocked down the elm tree in the front. Why, I just don't know how we'd manage around here if it wasn't for Neil. You know I think of him as a son and I always have." She sipped again and then peeked up at me with the raise of her elegant brow over the rim of her glass.

Unbelievable. I crossed my arms beneath my breasts and stared at my mother as if she'd grown a second head. Completely at a loss of how to respond, I gave up in disgust and headed to the bath for a very long soak in the tub.

I made sure to shout extra loud down the hall so she could hear me before I slammed the bathroom door. "Missed your calling, Mum! You should've been an actress on the stage!"

While the tub was filling, I rang my brother on my mobile.

"How's my baby sister?" He sounded quite cheery on the other end and I could hear background noise that sounded like he was probably in the pub.

"Fuck you, Ian."

"Yeah, well this is not the first time today I've heard that exact sentiment—"

"Not surprised, you arsehole!" I yelled, right before I hung up on him.

During my bath I had some time to think without other distractions getting in my way. The shock of seeing Neil again was powerful, and the hurt was still there.

Definitely still there.

Seeing him daily was going to be very hard on me. Oh God, how on earth would I do it? Could I do it? I didn't want to give up my job but thought I might have to.

I really didn't know anything about Neil's life since our break up, other than that he'd respected my wishes and never tried to come after me. He'd read my letter and done as I'd asked. How could he have left Cora after she was having his baby? I knew he wouldn't have been able to do it, and I was right. I'd seen her coming out of the clinic right before I was off for Italy and she was already showing, a nice little baby bump on her neat tidy figure. That was Neil's baby growing inside her. His child, who he would never abandon.

I didn't know he'd landed a fabulous job in London after the army. I'd always imagined he'd made a career in the military all these years, because he'd already achieved rank of captain last I'd known.

To be fair though, I'd told my mother and brother, that if they tried to interfere or pass along messages from or about Neil, I'd never forgive them for it. I'd announced my plans to be an *au pair* and said I wouldn't be sharing the details of our breakup, so not to ask. They had honored my wishes apparently. I'd known back then, that I'd never be able to hear all about his life after me, and survive. Letting him go, early in our relationship, had been the better choice for *my* survival. Moving on to a life without him had been terrifying and agonizing for me, but it was better than killing us both slowly.

I knew things about myself and about my feelings for Neil. Hell, I had the evidence of him, and what he'd meant to me tattooed on my back.

I knew I'd be unable to share him with Cora, or even his child, the instant she gave us her big reveal. No possible way I'd ever manage it. I am not perfect, but I'm honest about things I know to be fact. It would have killed me to stay, and I would have become bitter and vindictive, and destroyed Neil's love for me, anyway.

It was clear from his reactions that they'd been together and made a baby. He never denied it to me so I knew it was true. I forgave Neil that part of it. We weren't together when he slept with Cora, and he'd just come home from a long lonely tour. I understood. But, I also understood that Neil would never abandon a child that was his. I knew his character, and with the way he'd been abandoned by his father as a boy, he'd never do the same to his own.

I stood to get out of the tub and reached for a towel. As I did, I saw my cherry blossoms reflected in the mirror. On my back, right shoulder, where they would always stay. Why had I gotten it done?

Selfishness.

It was my little part of us to keep forever. Cherry blossoms in sky blue. *My* memory. Mine alone, that nobody could ever take away from me.

I hoped Neil was happy now. I truly wanted that for him, but it didn't change what I had to do for myself in order to survive the loss of him.

I knew what I knew. I'd have been completely unable to share him with Cora, no matter how limited their relationship. She would forever hold a piece of him, and I would covet that precious part of him that had been stolen from me. The familiarity Neil would have had to maintain with Cora surely would have poisoned our love and torn it down until there was nothing beautiful left. Just heartache. And, cruel jealousy. And hurt. I couldn't do that to Neil. He didn't deserve it after the childhood he'd lived through.

It made me a horrible person, true, but I could live with that understanding about myself. I was selfish when it came to love. I was selfish with Neil. And I just couldn't bear to endure the pain I would have brought to us both.

His child would be five years old now. I wondered about that baby. Boy or girl? Dark chocolate eyes with blonde hair, or more like Cora with her strawberry-blonde curls and light eyes? Had Mum and Ian met the child?

I finished drying off and hung up the towel. As I shrugged into my robe, I left the right shoulder off and studied my tat once more in the mirror. It was a beautiful piece of art. I had no regrets about having it now, or ever. My tiny little piece of Neil's love safely preserved in my skin.

The only bit I had left.

Despite the fact I wanted to kill him, I was at the bar drinkin' with him, regardless.

Ian set down his mobile and hung his head. "Everyone keeps telling me to sod off today. That was Elaina by the way."

So, Elaina was angry too. Well great, we had some common ground at least. We'd both had the earth ripped out from beneath us. I poked Ian in the shoulder.

"Why? Why the f-fuck did you bring her to BSI...? Why'd you do th-that?" Four pints in and I was really sopping drunk. Good thing I'd walked here because I sure as fuck wasn't able to drive. "Yer tryin' to kill me, brother?" I slurred another question at him.

Ian waved me off with his hand like I was a distracting gnat buzzing around his head. "The two of you are fuckin' ridiculous with your pining and your tats and your lost love. Get over it already, and do somethin' about it, why don't you." Ian narrowed his eyes to focus.

He was at least as drunk as me. "Mum and I couldn't stand either one of you anymore, so we helped you along a bit. Just a li'l bit o' help, is all."

"Well, that was fuckin' stupid of you then. She doesn't want anthin' to do with me, an' now we have t-to work t-together."

"No, yer fuckin' s-stupid. She's in love with you st-still. An' you are with her. I've seen yer cherry blossom tats an' how you are when the other person's name comes up." He tapped his head and nearly stabbed himself in the eyeball. "I see things. I know things."

I grabbed him by the collar of his shirt. "Don't you tell her about the tat or I'll b-b-bash you, Ian."

Ian's face cracked an enormous grin. "Yer such a fuckin' idiot. Ya don't know much do ya?"

"What tha bloody h-h-hell does that mean?"

"I'll let ya figure it out on yer own, b-brother, but I'll s-s-say this much…" He poked a finger into my forehead. "Yer not tha only one with a ch-cherry blossom t-tattoo.

The words of the song hit me like a brick to the head as I listened to Hendrix on Spotify. Music was part of my life and I couldn't imagine being without it, but today the lyrics fit too perfectly with the reality of what had happened with Elaina and me. It did nothing good for me. But make the ache more persistent.

A broom is drearily sweeping
Up the broken pieces of yesterday's life
Somewhere a queen is weeping
Somewhere a king has no wife
And the wind, it cries Mary

Not Mary. The wind was crying…Cherry.

I'd kept my distance at work from Elaina over the past few days. She'd done the same with me. It was strange, because for some reason, it wasn't as painful for me as I thought it would feel. Having her nearby was very soothing after so long of wondering where she was, how she was, what she was doing, who she was with. I finally knew the answers to all of those questions.

But, I also had new ones to ponder.

Ian's drunken confession in the pub had piqued my curiosity a lot. According to her brother, she had a cherry blossom tattoo somewhere on her body. Interesting. And why would Elaina do that?

I could only think of one reason why she would.

Same reason I'd gotten mine.

I dug around in my desk drawer until I found it. A flash drive of photographs I'd taken nearly six years ago. I made sure the door was locked of course, and told Susie to hold my calls.

The pictures loaded up in a slideshow format.

Nearly two hundred images: cherry blossoms, Elaina under the falling blossoms, selfies of us in the boat together, some close-ups of a blue dragonfly sitting on a cherry branch. I remembered the dragonfly photos specifically. I'd printed one out and taken it to the tattoo artist when she'd inked me, so she could get the design right.

Blue dragonfly in the cherry blossoms in an ancient Japanese tsuba design, sitting right on my chest over my beating heart.

I scrolled through the line of photos, one by one, remembering everything as the images loaded. Again, it was a strange sensation. I thought I had forgotten the memories, or at least hidden them away so deep that I wouldn't remember. But, that wasn't the case at all. The sights and sounds and emotions held in my memories, came right up to the surface in an instant, as easily as if our weekend at Hallborough had just happened.

I kept clicking the right arrow faster and faster until the series changed to times after we had returned home.

I stopped clicking and stared, unable to take my eyes away.

Elaina. Naked in my bed. Her eyes were on me, head tilted to the side, her beautiful hair splayed out, her perfect body soft and languid from being touched, kissed, and ravished by me only moments before.

I'd asked her if I could have some pictures of her like this to take with me and she had generously said yes. How strange to know that just hours later, our time together ended in the most heartbreaking way. A moment in time, captured in stunning images, that had meant my whole world on the day they were taken.

I clicked forward to the next picture, very aware that I had taken more than just the one. God, she was beautiful then. She was still beautiful, and inside this very building, where I was sitting right fuckin' *now!*

I could leave this office, go out to reception and look at her with my own eyes if I wanted to. I could ask her to dinner or out for lunch. I could get close enough to smell that heavenly perfume she wore, or shampoo she used on her hair, or whatever the hell it was that smelled so good when I got close. I could listen to her voice addressing me when I asked her a question. I could even reach out and touch her in a gesture socially acceptable for workmates.

I could do all of that.

If I wanted to.

I kept my arse in my desk chair and studied the naked pictures of her instead.

And thought about giving my cock a tug and using them to get me off.

17

For custom arrangements on display in reception, the florist delivered twice a week. I kept looking over at the magnificent creation, of what looked very much like cherry blossoms in a light blue vase. The long branches of pale pink blooms distracted me terribly. Was it possible that Neil had somehow requested them? They were so specific an arrangement... My Spidey senses were picking up on something with him, but I couldn't quite put my finger on it.

It was pretty apparent from the last few days, that he was avoiding me. I accepted why he would want to, but it still wasn't fun for me to sit at my desk and see him go by without saying much beyond a simple greeting. It made me very sad, but I didn't know what to do about it. And I didn't know how to make it any better for either of us. I was left wondering so much about what was on his mind.

I didn't see a wedding ring on his finger but that didn't confirm anything. Lots of men didn't wear them. I'd yet to be invited into his office so I'd not seen any pictures he might have of his family, or...Cora and their baby—

"So, how are you settling in? It is Elaina, right?"

My sad thoughts were interrupted by the boss who was leaning on the counter above my station with a coffee cup, flashing that handsome chiseled face at me with an extra dash of charm thrown in.

"Yes, Mr. Blackstone, I'm really enjoying this job a great deal."

"Oh, it's Ethan. We're very informal here in the office." He winked at me. "In fact, I don't mind if you call me E."

If I didn't know better I'd think he was flirting with me. Jesus, he was runway-model handsome. Women must fall at his feet regularly.

I laughed nervously. "My brother calls me E as well, but he's the only one."

"That's right. I knew that." He gave his head a tap with the heel of his hand. "Morrison is your brother. Good man to have a pint with, or three," he joked.

"Yeah, that's my brother all right, always willing to be somebody's drinking partner."

"It's never a good idea to drink alone," he said softly.

I nodded and smiled, unsure of how to respond.

"Well, I just wanted to give you a personal welcome and say that I've heard nothing but good things about what you're doing here for us. Keep up the good work, Elaina, and please, if you need anything don't hesitate to ask, okay?"

He smiled warmly but held his stare for a little too long to be just a friendly welcome. Yeah, it was an invitation all right. All I would have to do is let him know I was available and Mr. Blackstone would probably give me a time and a place.

"Okay...yes sir."

He tsk'd and cocked a brow at me. "Ethan, remember?"

"Ethan." I smiled, waiting for him to go.

Thankfully my switchboard lit up at precisely that moment. "Blackstone Security International, how may I direct your call?" The line was dead with dial tone only. A second call lit up the board almost immediately, and again I picked up.

Ethan lifted his coffee mug in a farewell salute, as I dealt with switching calls through, our little chat officially ended.

He punched in the key code and headed back through to the main offices. But as the door opened, I could see Neil standing just behind it, his mobile up to his ear. Ethan stepped around him, continuing in the direction down to his office, while Neil just stood there stonefaced. He stared me down from inside the doorway until it closed between us, cutting off our view of each other.

"Blackstone Security International, how may I direct your call?" I got dial tone again and frowned at my switchboard. Something weird was happening with the phone lines.

I thought about my short conversation with Ethan.

The boss was an interesting man. Besides being off-the-charts handsome, he was also very well-mannered and socially adept. But there was an edge to Ethan Blackstone that didn't quite fit. Something that didn't feel very mannerly, or even particularly social. I felt secure around him, yes, but this was a man who could do some serious damage to a woman if she was fool enough to let him. Make no mistake about it. I had no intentions of being that woman, so I wasn't worried in the slightest, but some girl would...someday.

I pushed my way into his office and got right up on him.

"Don't even think it."

Ethan pulled back a little and cocked a brow. "Don't think about what?"

"I'm not blind, you know," I scoffed. "I saw you on camera, flirting, swinging your cock around up front just now."

He narrowed his eyes at me. "What in the mother fuck are you railing on about, mate? Did you hit your head or something?" He opened his desk drawer where he kept his cigarettes.

I leaned over him, hands planted on the desk. "Not gonna happen. Not with her," I whispered right up against his face, my neck so tight it might snap.

"The new receptionist, you mean? Elaina?" He was eyeballing me by then.

"That's right. She's off limits, and you can tell that to your wandering cock and balls, too."

"Easy there, mate. I was just being polite." He lit up one of those Djarum Blacks he liked so well, the spice of clove scenting the air between us. "Making her feel welcome as a new member of the team is all. I'd not had a proper chance to do that yet."

He exhaled right in my face. Probably because I was still up on him, but it didn't deter me one iota. "Forget it, E. I'm warning you." I tilted my head and crossed arms over my chest to keep from doing something I would regret. "Leave off with Elaina. She's not going to be another of your one-night bang buddies. If you're in need, go find it somewhere else."

Ethan looked me over good, his blue eyes chilly as he took another drag on his ciggie. "You know her. I suppose you must since Morrison is her brother. Am I right?"

I managed a nod.

"You want to talk about it?" he asked carefully.

"No, I don't." I shook my head.

"Right, well, no worries then. I was only giving a welcome and being nice. You know I don't fraternize with employees on the job. I'd never do that to a subordinate."

"Not during working *hours* at least," I grumbled. I'd known E to tap an office girl or two, but to be fair, he'd only gone for the ones that worked away from the executive suite on one of the other floors.

Ethan snickered and leaned back in his chair, the cigarette hanging off his lip. "Are you all right, Neil?"

"No," I said, dropping myself into a chair opposite his desk.

We sat there in silence for a bit, him smoking, me breathing it in second hand, the smell reminding me of Afghanistan, taking me back to other times and other places. Places where I'd been with Ethan, a long time ago when things were different. He was very quick, and I imagined he'd puzzle it all out in another moment or two.

"Elaina's the girl, isn't she? The one from years ago,

that you…lost, right before that last tour." He lit up another Djarum.

"Yeah. She was the one."

I put on my coat and peered out the window from the forty-fourth floor.

Well, shit.

Late leaving work, and it was already completely dark outside. The fall weather had arrived in full force, too. The temperatures were dropping and the rain was falling.

The ride home on the train didn't worry me, but the walk to my house from the station most certainly did. Maybe I could call Mum to come pick me up in the car.

But I didn't like to do that. It was a risk I really couldn't take, and I knew very well why. Mum would be well into her G&T's by now.

I was pondering calling my brother, on the small chance he wasn't already committed to Friday night happy hour somewhere, when Neil stepped through to reception.

He wore a solemn look on his face and his coat on his back. With his briefcase in his hand, he appeared to be leaving work for the night, same as me.

"I'll take you home," he said, walking ahead of me toward the lifts.

I stared at him in surprise. This was the first time he'd really spoken to me since that first day, and it made me wary.

He stepped into the lift. I stayed rooted in the hall.

After a moment, he poked his head out, his hand holding the door open. "Well, are you coming?"

"What? No. I'll take the Tube like I always do."

He shook his head slowly at me. "You're not walking home in this pissing rain in the dark, Elaina."

"I'll ring Mum from the station to come and collect me."

"No, you won't ring her, and we both know why. Get in."

I paused, unsure how to respond, tempted by his direct command, but afraid to be so close to him again. The inside of a lift was very small quarters. And Neil was such a big man. And, he would be in it with me. Intimidating as hell was a good description for him at that moment.

"The lift, Elaina?" He cocked his head impatiently. The lift bell dinged and I saw the G lit up in red on the panel, indicating he was heading down to the parking garage.

"No, thank you." I shook my head at him. "I'm taking the Tube home." I let the doors close Neil inside the lift, where he was still frowning at me from behind those beautiful features he'd been born with.

Relief spilled through me and I closed my eyes for a moment.

With a steady hand, I calmly pressed the button to call another lift. When it arrived, I made sure to select the street level because I had a feeling Neil might insist on taking me home, despite my insistence otherwise.

He knew too much about me. He knew the station, and how far I had to walk from there in order to arrive at my home. He knew my mother's drinking habits and that she couldn't drive her own car to come for me. He knew Ian was busy somewhere, as it was a Friday night. Neil knew everything.

Elaina was living proof that it was very possible to want to protect someone and strangle them simultaneously. Metaphorical strangulation, of course, along with some other things I could think of doing to her.

Christ in heaven, I was going to lose my mind if I didn't spot her in the next minute or two.

Once she ditched me at the lifts it'd been a race across town to beat her train to the station. Not easy to do in Friday evening London traffic. Throw the rain in on top of it, and it was a bloody mess. The strangling still seemed a viable option to me at that moment. That, or kiss her until she couldn't breathe.

I had a trump card, though. I'd called her mum and tattled; right before assuring her I would find Elaina and bring her safely home. Mum Morrison still loved me even if her daughter didn't.

Yeah, it would make Elaina spitting mad but I didn't care. She could join my fuckin' hell club. I'd spent the past week in a continual state of madness from this whole cocked-up situation. She'd have to just deal with it. And me.

There she was, slogging through the sideways rain with her head down. I could spot those legs of hers anywhere. A hundred years could have passed, and my brain would still have remembered exactly how she was made.

I flashed my headlamps at her and pulled up beside the pavement.

She lifted her head in surprise as her eyes went wide.

I pushed open the passenger door.

"Get in."

She just stood there, her rain-soaked hair plastered against her face, challenging me.

"Did you call my mother, Neil?"

"I did indeed, now get in the car," I barked, ready to jump out and drag her in if I had to.

"That was stupid of you, then," she yelled, throwing her arm out.

"Not nearly as stupid as walking home in a torrential rainstorm, in the middle of the goddamn bloody night!"

She turned away and started walking again.

I saw red and it was all reaction after that. The Rover was up on the pavement blocking her path and she was looking at me like she wanted to slice off my balls and feed them to her pet alligator. "What is the matter with you, Neil?" she screeched.

"Right now, it's your stubbornness," I bit out. I pointed to the empty seat. "Now get your defiant arse into the MOTHERFUCKIN' SEAT OF MY CAR!"

She did it.

The interior of the Rover was silent except for the pounding of the rain. The earthy smell of water filled the air and mixed with the scent of her hair and wet coat. I think we were both in shock.

I'm sure I'd never shouted so loudly before to any person. These extreme emotions were starting to get to me. I was the guy who kept his cool and a level head. I didn't even recognize myself anymore.

I looked over at Elaina sitting beside me, her arms folded across her chest, hair dripping, eyes straight ahead, and so utterly beautiful even in this bedraggled state, that it hurt to have her so close. It hurt because she was still so far away from me and I didn't know how to make her let me back in.

Her mobile rang from inside her coat pocket. She rolled her eyes as she pulled it out and answered the call.

"Yes, Mum. I'm with Neil right now and he's bringing me home." She paused listening. "I'll tell him. Okay. Bye."

I couldn't imagine what she was thinking. She wasn't talking and she wasn't fighting me either, she just sat there in the front seat of my Rover, so very still.

I reached over her for the belt to buckle her in and could see she was shivering.

"You're cold." I cranked up the heat and backed off the pavement, straightening out the wheels and parking it up against the curb. The windscreen wipers methodically passed back and forth between us.

"M-mum w-wants you to s-stay for dinner," she chattered blankly, still staring forward out into the dark rainy night.

But what about you, Elaina?

"I'm sorry for screaming at you," I said softly.

I wished she'd look at me, but she wouldn't…or

couldn't after our terrible shouting match.

And so, I just sat there and watched her, the heater inside the car working overtime, making the air warmer by the minute.

"It's okay," she said finally, wiping one side of her face with her fingers. Was she crying?

"Elaina...look at me, please." I waited while time seemed to slow down to a crawl.

She turned her head toward me, her chin up and trembling like she was guarding herself from falling apart.

"I didn't know you worked there. I wouldn't have taken the job if I'd known. They tricked me into it, and I just don't want you to think I did this on purpose—"

I cut her emotional ramble off with two fingers to her lips. "I know. I know it was them and not you. Don't you worry about that."

She froze when I touched her, looking fragile enough to shatter at any second.

I dropped my hand away, but I didn't want to. I wanted to run it around the back of her neck and draw her up against me. I still wanted her. Despite everything that had happened between us, all of the betrayal and abandonment—my heart just didn't care about any of it.

Elaina was here. My Cherry Girl was here right beside me.

18

Neil drove me home. I was numb and it wasn't from the cold rain. Subdued was a good word to describe how we both were after that blow up on the pavement. I'd never seen Neil lose his temper like that. So angry. He'd driven his car up *onto* the pavement for Christ's sake.

He pulled into the drive of my house and I found the courage to ask him.

"Are you coming in? Mum wants you to stay."

He turned and met me head on, his big hands still gripping the steering wheel. "What about you, Elaina? Do you want me to stay?"

"Well, is it—is it all right for you to be here?"

He looked puzzled by my question.

"What?"

He wasn't going to make this easy on me apparently. I swallowed and went for it.

"Are you married?"

His eyes widened for an instant. "Come again?"

"Don't make me ask that again, please."

He paused for a minute before responding, as if he really needed to choose the right words. "I'm going to chalk that one up to the fact you're not yourself right now. You're soaked through to the skin, and we've had a row that's upset both of us—but did you just ask me if I'm married?"

"Yes," I whispered.

He scoffed and shook his head, looking away from me now and out the window. "No. I'm not married."

"So you and Cora didn't stay together?"

He flipped back toward me. "Umm, no," he said slowly, shaking his head again, his lips slightly parted.

"Why didn't you, Neil?"

"I didn't want to, Elaina."
Fear had started to bloom in the pit of my stomach

and I suddenly felt ice cold again. "But the b-baby…I saw Cora after you left. She was pregnant and showing. I saw with my own eyes." While Neil sat glaring at me, a thought rushed through my mind. *Oh no.* "Did she lose it?"

"No, she didn't lose it. She had a son." Neil had turned away again, as if he couldn't stand the sight of me. He was answering my questions while speaking to the window and looking out at the rain.

"Oh. What's his name?"

"I don't know. I only saw him one time and she didn't tell me."

"You don't—you don't see your son?" This wasn't the man that I knew. I didn't understand any of this. Why didn't he see his son or even know his name?

He turned back to me once more and told me why, his eyes full of sadness I could read clearly even from the dim light inside his car. "I don't see him, because he is not mine."

I shuddered as a chill rushed through my whole body and froze me. I was speechless for a moment, unable to speak, afraid to look at him. Terrified for what else I'd see in his eyes.

I don't see him, because he is not mine.

"But—but she said—I saw you with the doctor scan…You never denied it…"

I don't see him because he is not mine.

"I wrote you a letter. I told you I understood why you had to be with Cora…"

Neil didn't react at first. He just looked at me, his expression growing darker and darker as understanding dawned for both of us. I realized why he was so angry.

I don't see him, because he is not mine.

"Oh, God." I slammed a hand over my mouth, trying to quiet the rising panic flooding me.

As if that would work.

Involuntary reactions, nothing more.

He still hadn't said anything. Neil was letting me do all the talking, giving me plenty of rope to hang myself on.

"If he wasn't your baby, then why…why didn't you say something? You let me go and didn't tell me…Neil— please say this wasn't all for nothing."

I could feel the hysteria letting loose. The truth dawning on me with such brutal force I could barely breathe.

I don't see him, because he is not mine.

He leaned in very close and grabbed me by the shoulders, forcing me to own up to my horrifying mistake, gripping tightly and shaking me a little with every sharp bite of each word he spoke.

"Why did *you* leave without ever giving me a chance to tell you anything? You just left me there on the eve of my deployment. You let *me* go. Didn't you love me enough to even listen at all, Elaina? Was I not worth even that much to you?"

I closed my eyes as my heart collapsed in on itself. My tragically grievous error now apparent, I had nowhere to escape. What had I done? I'd been the cause of so much needless pain for the both of us, all because I'd been afraid to listen, and to share any part of him with anyone else.

Silent tears poured out of me as I tried to find the words. "No, no, noooo." I sobbed, "I saw her pregnant—we all believed it was your baby...even you believed it..." I lost the ability to say any more. What could I say to him, anyway? What words were there to offer?

Very few. Actually, none at all.

I'd not stayed around to find out the truth back then, why should he believe anything I said to him now? I couldn't fathom why Neil was even beside me at this very moment, giving a thought to my needs, and seeing me safely home at night. I didn't deserve it from him. He must be doing it only out of a sense of devotion to my family, after all, they'd never let him go. I had been the only one to do that.

I spoke. The words came out of me and they were all I had to give to him. Words. Bitter sawdust in my mouth—that gave no comfort, only more pain—in the realization of what all this really meant about me and him, and our long years apart.

"You were worth it, Neil. You were. I wasn't though. I—I—I am so sorry..."

He closed his eyes, still holding onto me, as if he couldn't bear to hear the confession of my regret.

From somewhere deep inside me, a source of adrenaline started pumping because I pulled out of his tight grip and got the hell out of his car. I bolted.

Running was something I was really good at.

I managed to stumble inside the house, ignoring my mother's comments about trying to walk home alone in a storm, her inquiry about Neil, and wasn't he having dinner with us? I don't know what I said to her.

I reached the safety of my bedroom, somehow. A sanctuary of sorts. A place where I could weep in solitude, and in peace. I'd figure out what to do tomorrow.

I just wanted to sleep and grieve for what I had done to him. To us.

To even accept it, hurt so much, I was afraid to close my eyes for fear of what my dreams would be like once I finally slept.

I had to see for myself. There are some things a woman cannot take on good authority and this was one of them. I had to see her and ask her why she'd done it. She may not tell me, and more pain was surely coming my way for my efforts, but I had to ask.

I stood on a street, looking at a house in a Barnet neighbourhood, the address of which I'd pried out of my brother. The house, where Cora lived with her husband.

Just as I was about to cross the street, the door opened and out came a mother with two small children. A little boy holding her hand, and a younger girl in pink, riding in a pram. It was her. Cora looked mostly the same, maybe not quite as fit as before she'd given birth to two kids, but it was her.

I followed them to the park.

It didn't take long to understand how apparent it was that Neil was not the father of her son. The children were very dark with skin that couldn't have come from Neil and his Anglo DNA. At one point, the boy came over to where I sat on my bench and dug around in the sand pit with some toys. He was a handsome little lad, but not Neil's son. This little boy's father was Black.

"I thought it was you sitting here." Cora had spotted me and made her way over. "I heard you'd returned to England."

I stared up at her and asked one word. "Why?"

She sat down on the bench beside me.

"Why did I tell Neil that my little Nigel belonged to him? That's a story that you won't like to hear, I'm afraid."

"Tell me anyway," I said, numbly. Here it was. The truth behind everything I'd sacrificed on the back of a lie and my fear of losing my heart.

"I'm not proud of what I did to him. Having children of your own changes your perspective on things, though. I've learned a lot since. But basically it came down to survival."

"Survival, Cora? Who's survival?"

"I needed money and Denny Tompkins came along at just the right moment for it. He hated Neil for taking you away from him. I told Denny I was knocked up and without any good prospects, and that you and Neil could just sod off together in lover's land. He offered me a tidy sum to show my scan to Neil, and to tell him the baby was his. I did my part and Denny made good on the payment."

"So, I left Neil over a lie." It wasn't a question I was asking. Just greater understanding of what I had done.

Cora was still beside me. No harsh words or gloating, she only shared the bare simple truths.

"Denny didn't make out so well, though. You wouldn't take him back and a few months later you went away to Spain."

"Italy...I went to Italy." Even the sound of my own voice was nearly unrecognizable to my ears.

Cora kept talking. "Wherever you went, you were gone, so Denny didn't ever get you back. I owed it to

Neil to tell him though, and I did that as soon as I could. He even saw us in the market once and gave his regards. It all worked out. Nigel married me and we had little Allison not two years after Nigel Jr., so yeah, it all worked out in the end."

"It didn't work out for me," I said, staring out at all the busy children and parents in the park.

"So, why didn't you ever ask him about it then? Neil would have told you what I told him, that the baby wasn't his." I could tell she was staring at me with a puzzled expression.

So simple a question. Why didn't I ever ask him? Why didn't I stay and try to work it out with him? Why didn't I ever give Neil the chance to tell me what had really happened?

"I don't know," I whispered.

I watched it all. I followed her at a distance and surveyed her visit to the park with Cora. I was still trailing her, curious as to where she was off to. It probably made me a sick bastard, but I was stalking Elaina and had no intentions of stopping.

Thank Christ Ian had rang me to say what he thought his sister was up to. She wanted Cora's address and that meant Elaina was going to confront her.

Observing their exchange in the park surprised me, though. I read their lips through some of the conversation thanks to the high powered lenses I was privy to in my line of work. The surprising part was precisely how non-confrontational their exchange was. No screaming catfight for me to break up. No hair pulling or gloves thrown down. Nothing. They were both very well behaved throughout the whole thing. At the end of it, Cora asked her a question about me. I could tell she asked her a question because I got the words *why* and *Neil* clearly, through reading her lips.

Elaina answered her very shortly with just a word or two. And then, she got up off the bench and left the park. I saw her brush at her eyes a few times. Her head was down in the autumn wind, a long, trailing blue scarf blowing back away from her body as she walked.

She looked to be crying and it was easy to see she was upset, but I left her alone. She would resent what I was doing, and I would've too if the tables were turned. We were both private people.

I watched her walk to the nearest Underground station and go down to the trains.

There was no choice but to follow in the Rover and make a guess as to where she might end up. I texted Ian and told him to ring her and find out for me.

I had to be there for her. I *was going* to be there for her.

There was no place else for me to be.

19

I vowed to never set foot in *The Racehorse* again. Never. Bad things had happened there. The worst sort of decisions had gone down inside these old walls. I'd lost so much, and gained so little, from encounters in the little Hampstead pub tucked away in the community where I'd grown up.

I gestured to Bert behind the bar for a refill and drank while waiting for him to show up.

It took a bit of time, but eventually he got there. I heard his motorbike pull up first, and that's how I knew he'd arrived.

The swagger in his step, the self-satisfied smirk on his face, both were very telling of what he thought my invite was all about. What misconceptions poor Denny was under.

"Hey gorgeous, I have to say that getting your text absolutely topped my day." He buzzed my cheek and sat down beside me at the bar.

I took a gulp of wine and looked him over. "Really. And why's that?"

He leaned in close to me, his long hair falling over his forehead in a rakish wave, the looks of which helped to serve his bad boy image, I suppose. Through all the intervening years since my time with Denny, I could say the whole concept he had going on, did absolutely nothing for me anymore.

I smiled a little…and held myself back from reaching out and squeezing my hands around his neck until he choked.

He spoke low and close. "I'll take you back to my place and show you if you like."

"Ahh, an invitation…other girls should be so lucky."

"You can be, baby. Just like old times."

"Old times, Denny?"

"Yeah, before you ran away, baby." He wagged a finger at me. "You should have never run away. You made me pretty lost, when you took off for Europe—"

As Denny blabbed and spewed his twisted notion of me out of his too pretty lips, I felt myself centering. All of my energy and focus boiled together into a white hot rage that had to find an outlet somehow. To hold it inside any longer, probably would have killed me. I was able to control the rage initially, waiting for my moment, but once he said those words out loud, *you should have never run away,* I truly lost my mind.

Denny was right, you see. I should have never run away.

I ran away from Neil when I should have stayed.

An out of body experience is a strange sensation. You feel very detached and the sounds in the room become muted. Your body floats above the ground and you can see everything so clearly. It happened to me at the bar. I knew it was happening and I welcomed the altered state of my reality with open arms.

I watched myself calmly from above as I morphed into something rather animalistic, a demon that resembled me, pounding away on Denny Tompkins. Anywhere on his body where I could make contact was satisfactory. I hit, and slapped, and scratched. I tried to rip his hair out of his scalp. My red wine was thrown, along with my purse, and whatever else I could get my hands on to hurl at him.

I could hear a woman screaming in an otherworldly cry. She didn't even sound human, but the terrible pain and anguish she felt was clear to anyone that heard it.

Eventually, I realized that the woman was me.

Denny got in one good defense blow, once the

surprise of my attack was over. He shoved me off him and sent me sprawling down to the floor, my body sliding backward, taking out chairs and stools from the force of the fall.

"Get off me you crazy cunt!" he screamed, welts from my scratches rising up on his skin, blood trickling the corner of his mouth. "What the fuck is wrong with you, you fuckin' whore?!"

"You know what it's for! You earned it for what you paid Cora to do to Neil. You paid her to lie to us about the baby. I hope you rot in hell, you filthy, degenerate, cocksucker!"

He drew his fist back to strike me but he never got the chance. Neil clocked him in the jaw, which took Denny Tompkins down. One punch. Out cold, on the scarred floor of The Racehorse.

Neil scooped me up and carried me out of there. He buckled me into his Rover and drove us away. I cried in the seat beside him and fell into absolute despair.

With each tear that fell, the weight of my anguish grew heavier.

Neil didn't ask anything of me. He didn't say anything at all beyond a quick check to see if I was injured. "Are you hurting anywhere?"

Only my heart. "No. I'm fine. The calm after the storm."

I didn't say another word to Neil after that, not even a thank you for taking out Denny before he could strike me.

He let me be and drove us to my mother's house.

When he came around to open my door and helped me out, I was grateful, because I was suddenly so exhausted I wasn't sure I would make it on my own two feet.

I didn't have to worry about that, either.

Neil carried me inside my house.

I had to shut my eyes. It hurt too badly to be so close up against him, to feel his muscles, to smell his scent, to look at his beauty, and know that I had given it all away. Given it all away for a lie.

He laid me on my bed after pulling off my jacket and scarf. He took off my boots and tucked a coverlet over me. I allowed Neil to take care of me because I was physically unable to do any of it for myself at that moment.

I rolled onto my side and burrowed under the warm blanket. I slept.

The sound of laughter woke me from my sleep back from the dead. I heard Neil talking with my mother. The smooth deep roll of his voice was unmistakable to me. Just something I knew which was buried deep into my memories of the house and our time spent in it together.

He'd been there so many times, and helped cook so many dinners, that hearing him gave me a feeling of nostalgia— comfort, from such long known and welcomed memories.

So, he'd stayed after my meltdown with Denny? I couldn't imagine why he had. Maybe Mum had pressed him to stay and eat since he wasn't able to the night before.

Don't think about that night.

I checked my bedside clock.

I'd been asleep for four hours. What in the hell had they been doing for all of that time I wondered. Well, no, scratch that. I didn't want to know. The two of them were peas in a pod and they always had been. My mother and Neil had no problem spending time together, period.

I hauled myself out of bed and into the bathroom. Bloody hell, I looked a fright. Like a cross between a bush baby and Lily Munster: my eyes were so wide, and my skin so pale.

This repair job was gonna take an extra minute or two.

I went to work on brushing my teeth, washing my face and combing out the rat's nest camouflaged within my hair. I decided on some yoga pants, and a long pink jumper with blue piping at the neck, hem and sleeves. It was really soft and I could sort of hide in it which was exactly the look I was going for at that moment. I pulled my hair up into an untidy knot and shoved my feet into my baby-blue UGGs.

In fact, I'd love nothing more than to hide in my room for the next week, but I knew my mother, and she would *never* allow such a thing. Not when we had a guest in our home. I was surprised she hadn't already been in to drag me out.

"Elaina?" She tapped on my door and called through.

Think of the devil and she appears as if by magic.

"I'll be out directly, Mum." I answered.

I sprayed on a spritz of Light Blue by D&G and took a deep breath.

Time to face the music. Or rather, the Mummy and McManus foodie show.

I followed the sound of their chattering down the hall and into the kitchen. *Huge surprise there.* My inner sarcasm was going to have to take a back seat for a bit, I realized. This was not the time or place to let loose with it.

I watched them for a moment, working together from the doorway. I had to admit, they were rather adorable as I listened in on their conversation. Neil had called her Mum for years and years, and was as much of a son to her as Ian. This was very apparent to me as I eavesdropped and observed, both of them wearing matching chef aprons, Mum with her hi-ball glass of G&T, and Neil with his Guinness.

I headed for the coffee pot and the cup cupboard.

"How was your sleep?" he asked to my back, as I dumped sweetener into my coffee.

"Very much needed," I said, shielding myself behind the enormous mug and taking a sip of scalding sweet coffee.

Mum came over and felt my forehead with the back of her hand. "Darling, I hope you're not ill with some horrible flu. Probably didn't help you were out walking in the freezing rain last night."

I ignored her reminder about the very traumatic events of the previous evening. I could only take so much. The night's revelation had gotten me out onto the proverbial ledge and ready to jump. After what Cora revealed, when we spoke in the park, I was barely clinging on by my fingernails.

"No worse for wear, Mum," I lied, pressing a kiss to her cheek.

I plastered on my best smile and beamed it in Neil's direction, faking my cheerfulness all the way.

"What are you two concocting for our dinner? Sounded like quite the party going on in here." I made a face. "In fact, you woke me up with it."

Neil leaned up against the butcher block counter and studied me. Totally relaxed in his jeans and long sleeved black shirt with the sleeves pushed up. Such a beautiful man. He'd grown into his big body—even more handsome with the added years of maturity than he'd been when he was younger. His hair was lighter than I remembered though, as if he bleached the ends. He had a new tattoo on his forearm, too. I knew exactly what it was as soon as I saw it. Jimi Hendrix's signature. So very Neil to get that inked on to his skin.

It wasn't easy to see him like that and not remember what that body looked like without the clothes. And when he was making love to me with it.

Okay, that hurt. I gave myself an emphatic and harsh mental slap on the hand. No more wandering thoughts about the past or what I'd walked away from. I couldn't indulge or I'd never make it, and Mum and Ian would be visiting me at Bethlem Hospital where I'd be wearing a tight white coat with a very long belt.

"Well if you didn't wake up you'd never be able to get to sleep tonight," he said, taking a drink of his Guinness.

"Right," I said dismissively. "So what are we having?" I peered toward the oven. "Whatever's in there smells divine." I inhaled.

"That's Mum's perfect roast beef and potatoes," Neil told me.

"Oh, but Neil went out and bought the nicest piece of beef while you were sleeping, Elaina. He's thought of everything, even a lovely dessert he's going to make for us later," Mum chattered cheerfully.

"Ahh, nice. What will you make?" I asked.

"Fool."

"That sounds…umm…interesting?—I think."

He laughed. "A fool is nothing more than cooked fruit stirred into freshly whipped cream. Easy, right? If I can make it, then anyone can."

"And tell Elaina what the cooked fruit is, dear," Mum told him with barely suppressed glee.

"Oh, yeah, I thought about it and decided to go with…cherries." He gave me a boyish grin and pursed his lips together to keep from laughing outright.

I rolled my eyes. "Funny. You two are absolutely hilarious together. Make sure to top my portion of *Fool* with extra fruit, please."

The act I was playing would be difficult to maintain for much longer before I snapped. *It was all fun and games until somebody got hurt,* just as the old saying went. I could only march in step for so long before I fell out of formation. The more attention he paid me—the sweet gentle teasing, the kind remarks, the smiles and winks—the worse I felt. It just taught me more about what I'd left behind. What I'd never really have for myself again.

Oh, it was nice that we could be civil to one another now. The über awkwardness was behind us it seemed, but how was I supposed to just go forward with Neil? Former lovers now friends? And for how goddamn long could I stand it? Working at BSI was going to be torture. I should probably start searching for another job.

The utter emptiness inside me, the lack of motivation to find anything remotely good about this scenario with Neil and me, had just up and died.

Later, after dinner had been cleared away and we were onto our Cherry Fool, which had turned out very nice, the fun and games just got more massively surreal.

"Neil darling, tell Elaina all about your wonderful inheritance."

"Oh, I'm sure she doesn't want to hear about that, Mum," he said, focusing on his creamy dessert as a way to avoid the topic.

My ears perked up instantly. Again, I'm the last person on earth to know things about Neil, and the details of his life. But whom did I have to blame for that? I breathed and told my fluttering heart to settle down and start getting used to it.

"Yes, I do," I blurted.

"Yes, she does," Mum said, speaking at the same time as me.

Neil's eyes softened as he looked up at me and I knew what he was on about.

You're trying to gentle the blow because you know how badly I'm struggling with this.

He knew me so well.

"You've gotten an inheritance? But from whom?"

"A great uncle I'd never met. He was the brother of

my gran. No living children and I was his closest blood relative." He shrugged. "Nobody was more surprised than me."

"When did this happen?" *Stupid question to ask him. You know the answer.*

"While I was still deployed." He shifted his body in the chair. "The solicitors had to wait on me to come home. It was months before I could get up there to see the place."

If I'd stuck around I could have helped him while he was gone.

"Yes, and Neil has a beautiful house on an estate in Scotland, Elaina. There's a good deal of land for hunting and a lake where you can fish from a boat. Ian's been up there with him on hunting weekends before. The land is so stunning in photos…oh, and tell her about the cherry trees, darling."

He looked uncomfortable while Mum gushed about the lovely Scottish country estate that everyone in the world knew he owned, but me, apparently.

I set down my spoon and focused on him, giving him my full attention and a smile. Somehow, I knew what was coming would be painful to hear. Premonitions happen sometimes and this one was gonna sting.

"There are cherry trees on the property," he began. "An unusual variety that blooms twice in a year. In the early spring of course, but in autumn, after all the leaves have changed their colours and fallen down…they come into bloom for a second time. They call it Autumn

Cherry."

That's not fair.

When he finished speaking, I blinked to keep my eyes from flooding. I thought I did a pretty good job considering the words that had just come out of his mouth, and the hidden meaning within them. *They come into bloom for a second time.*

"It sounds very lovely. I hope to see pictures some time. And congratulations, I'm so happy for your good fortune."

He nodded his head in acknowledgement.

I pushed my chair out and got up from the table with a smile...I think. I was certainly trying my hardest to pull it off anyway.

"You know...I'm going to have to excuse myself for the night." I brought my hand up to my temple. "My head is just pounding something awful and I think the best thing for me is to just give it up and get back in bed."

Neil's soulful eyes rested on me as I babbled away; no judgment, none of the harsh anger I'd seen in them before, just kindness and acceptance. I couldn't look into them anymore. Too painful to realize I would never be the recipient of those eyes looking at me out of love.

"Mum, Neil, thank you for the smashing meal. It was superb. Goodnight."

Neil pulled up to his feet in deference to me

standing, his manners still functioning perfectly after all the years of training by his gran.

"It was my pleasure."

I turned and left the dining room. I held myself together until I was just in the doorway—when I heard him say it.

"Feel better, Cherry."

My legs actually gave out enough to cause me to lose step when he said it. Like the slice of a blade across the back of my Achilles. Or across my heart.

I would have made it safely out of there if he hadn't called me Cherry.

Damn you, Neil McManus.

20

Elaina avoided me like the plague during the following week. I watched her carefully to see if I could make a crack in that armor she'd built up, but had very little success. She would talk to me, and that was about it.

I left things on her desk when she was away from it. I'd offer to take her home after work hoping I could get her alone for an hour or two and make some real progress, but she ditched me at times when I was unable to leave, or made Ian drive her.

I didn't give up, though. I had some hope you see.

I'd been there when she'd learned the truth about Cora and me, and seen what the revelation had done to her. The truth—opposed to what she'd believed all these years—had devastated her.

Elaina had rage, anger and great regret brewing inside her over our break up. I'd seen her go after Tompkins and witnessed the raw fury that possessed her when she was told about the alliance between Cora and Tompkins to break us apart. I'd never known about their illicit deal, and it was probably a very good thing, because I would be locked up for murder had I known, no doubt.

The attack at the pub had been the great leveler, an event which opened everyone's eyes to what had really happened, and to the choices that had been made nearly six years ago. By her. By me. Elaina wasn't the only one at fault. I'd not gone after her or forced her to see the truth when I should have done. I allowed her to believe a lie because my pride was too great to take the fall on the idea that someone who loved me could just let me go like that.

Yeah, the scars from the past are cocksuckin' motherfuckers, aren't they?

But I figured something out about her and me. I learned that regret gets you nothing but a bigger pile of shit to shovel around. And so, I made a decision. I decided not to muck around in the regret shit pile for even one more day.

It was impossible for Elaina to convey an aura of not caring about me anymore, when I'd seen her, with my own eyes, try her damnedest to kill the man responsible for tearing us apart.

Being optimistic with the hope that she still loved me did not seem like such a stretch anymore.

Now all I needed to do was to convince her of it.

I'd arranged for some subtle hints, like the florist arrangements in reception, but cherry blossoms in blue vases weren't going to cut it and send her back into my arms, or my bed. Not with the way she was locked down so tight. I believed we could get past the hurt and misconceptions. I believed we could love each other again. If I wanted her in my life, then I needed to step up my game.

And my Cherry Girl needed a push.

Earlier in the week, a notice had been delivered from the Personnel department for me to report for scheduled self-defense training. The gist of the email was this: all employees were required to take a basic course in self-defense maneuvers. As BSI provided security for high profile clientele, one could never assume a lunatic wouldn't show up with grievances. To that end, all staff must be thoroughly trained in defense to be prepared in the event of such an incident.

What a pleasant thought. Especially as my desk was the first line of defense for said lunatic if they came to see us via the forty-fourth floor. *They better teach me some damn good moves then.*

At lunch that day, Frances gave me directions of how

to get to the training facility and what to expect. I checked my watch. Three more hours.

All week I'd had Neil up my arse demanding I allow him to take me home. I'd always said no, or tried to find an alternative through Ian. If the weather cooperated, I brought good shoes for walking in my bag and changed at the station. Unfortunately, the weather was not my friend at the moment. Pouring rain and very cold, just like the night Neil and I had our blow up. The reminder of that night put me in a very foul mood, and because I knew he'd insist on taking me home, anyway.

Aaaand, there was his email sitting in my inbox when I got back from lunch.

TO: emorrison@bsiltd.co.uk
No ditching me today. I'm driving you home. N

I had a legitimate excuse to use on him though, and that made me grin as I replied to his message. I was not going to allow him to bully me over it. Quite frankly, I didn't even know what he was doing lately. Leaving coffees and treats on my desk when I stepped away. Emails. Texts. He had to be watching me on a security cam in order to know when I left my station. *Privacy much, Neil?* And what a waste of his workday. I was thoroughly annoyed with him.

TO: nmcmanus@bsiltd.co.uk
No, I can't. Have a required self-def. training class today after work. E

Take that, Mr. Overbearing, I thought as I pressed 'send.'

My victory was very short lived.

That and the fact he must've been sitting at his desk with his email open because he replied almost instantly.

TO: emorrison@bsiltd.co.uk
I'll wait for you to finish your class then.

His response made me angry and I told myself I wasn't going to stand for it another second. I kept reminding myself of that as I left my station and passed through the doors. I marched my way straight down to his office.

His secretary, Susie, smiled at me as I passed by her desk. I smiled back and said hello, as if it were the most normal thing in the world to storm into Neil's office with intent to murder him. *No apologies for speaking the truth.*

Then I barged in.

His head snapped up from where he'd been studying his computer screen. Probably composing another direct command to me via email.

"No, you won't." I said tightly, my arms folded beneath my breasts.

The corner of his mouth turned up a little as if I amused him. It made me want to smack it off him.

"Oh I most definitely will, Elaina," he said very softly.

His jaw ticked and his eyes roved over me leisurely.

From the strappy black heels on my feet, up my legs, over my body, to linger in the vicinity of my breasts a little longer than the rest, and then kept going north until he rested them on my face. The look he gave me was one of pure, abandoned, dirty, sex. I could feel it crackling in the air between us and the effect was one that rendered me wet between my legs and struggling for breath in an instant. If he tried anything with me I was doomed. I swallowed and tried to hold back the shiver threatening to reduce me to a quivering mass on his office floor.

He saw everything.

This was bad.

"Why—why are you doing this to me, Neil?"

"Doing what? Driving you home so you don't have to walk in the rain?"

"Yes! No, I mean—I mean why are you doing *this*?"

"This?"

"Don't be an arsehole for making me say it."

"Sorry, babe, but being an arsehole suits me right now. What is the *this* that's bothering you so much?"

"Neil…please. Stop. I—can't take it from you day in and day out."

"But you're wrong about that, beautiful girl. You *can* take it." He winked. "And you still haven't told me what the *this* is, Elaina." He tilted his head at me then, now the one with folded arms.

I can't take him calling me beautiful girl *and winking at me, I do know that much!* I so needed to get the hell out of his office. And fast.

"Well, I'm waiting."

He was going to make me say it, the bastard. What was wrong with him at the moment, anyway?

"Pursuing me at work every day like it matters," I finally yelled. "If you don't want m-me—then why are you on me every goddamn day?"

Oh, God. Did I just ask him that?

He stood up from his desk and took a step in my direction. He didn't say anything as he stalked forward. I don't know what he intended to do when he got to me, but the instinct to run flashed through my head. Neil looked like a dangerous predator, and I felt pretty much like helpless prey.

"What are you doing?" I demanded, backing up until I was pressed against the wall.

He just kept coming at me until I was penned in, his arms blocking an exit on either side of my shoulders.

"I'm showing you that running away is not gonna work anymore, Elaina." He brought his face up close to my neck and inhaled. "Mmmmm…you don't really want to run from me now, anyway. I can smell it."

Dear. Lord.

I shook my head at him trying to ward off the intoxication from his bloody scent of pure male domination that did far more to render me useless than alcohol ever could.

"What do you want from me?" I whispered up against his stubbly jaw, my lips so close, I could press them against his skin with barely any effort. I couldn't hold back the whimper that escaped me.

He removed one hand from the wall and touched between my breasts with the backs of two fingers. He drew them up slowly, dragging them along my sensitive skin, higher until he reached my throat, and then my neck, up my jaw, and then finally to my lips.

I was so aroused; I probably could have an orgasm if he told me to. It wouldn't take much for me to arrive at that blissful place with him. It had been so long since we'd been together, but my body remembered. All. Too. Well.

He pushed his two fingers into my mouth. I let him.

"I want *this*, Cherry."

He brought his lips very close to mine, his fingers still on my tongue, probing, slick from my saliva.

"I want this mouth screaming my name when I'm inside you and you're about to come. I want you in my bed so we can fuck all night long...over and over until you're a slave to it—just as you used to be."

My eyes rolled back in my head, and I was really

grateful for the wall because I would have slid down to the floor in a boneless heap if it wasn't bracing me.

I had her exactly how I wanted her. Hot, sexed, and submissive. Better than I remembered. And, bloody fuckin' hell if I wasn't out of my mind with wanting, barely coherent of what I said to her. Or did.

It was *on* with my Cherry, once again.

The flowery scent of her skin wound me up something fierce to the point I could think of nothing else but getting my cock into her. I was going for it right then with her in my office. And the fuckin' desk would just have to do. In a few minutes, it would become a literal fuckin' desk.

I was figuring what the best maneuver would be to get her from the wall to where I could make a place to lay her out in all her cherry-haired glory, so I could push my way back in. And make her see what was so clear to me. She wanted me, too. I knew she did, down deep in my bones.

Oh yeah, the vision was all coming together in my mind beautifully. Me picking her up and hauling her over onto my desk. My fingers finding the button that locked the goddamn door so nobody would interrupt. My mouth on her throat making its way down to savor breasts that tasted sweeter than honey. My palms pushing up the tight black skirt that caressed her arse, before moving them along to the inside of thighs I would spread wide for—

Ethan busted into my office and ruined everything.

Motherfuckin' cunt of the world!

"Look at what's just arrived, mate. I had to come tell you in person. It's fucking amazing—" Ethan cut off whatever he was saying mid-speech, and backed out of the door, muttering something about coming back later.

Yeah, you do that, E.

I might just have to kill him now.

While I was mentally eviscerating Ethan for his untimely visit, Elaina made good her escape. She gave a little squeak, ducked under my arm and took off. I tried to hold her back but she was too fast and had just enough leeway to skirt the other way and bolt.

My hand snatched at empty air.

But I could still smell her. The gentle flowery scent that I loved, above all others, was still present in the room even when she wasn't.

I went over to my desk and sat down slowly. Slow was the operative word, due to the state of my cock. The goddamn thing was so hard by that point, I could have used it to punch in the numbers to dial up Personnel.

"BSI Personnel Department, Helen speaking, how may I direct you?"

"Helen, this is Neil. I need to know who's on the board for self-defense training for Elaina Morrison, today at five."

"That would be Terrence, Mr. McManus."

"Thank you, Helen. Just need to free up some bodies and tweak the timing a bit. You've been very helpful."

I dialed again.

"Terrence Shaw, here."

"Terrence, this is Neil. I'm going to have to pull you off the SD training for Elaina Morrison. You're scheduled for five o'clock today. We need you on another job."

"All right, boss. Just tell me where you want me and what time," Terrence replied easily.

Good man, that Terrence. Might need to see he gets a nice bonus at Christmas for being so agreeable.

"Right. Well something's come up that is definitely taking priority for today. Miss Morrison will just have to be rescheduled for sometime next week. Got a pen?"

I ended the call with Terrence and leaned back in my chair, feeling pretty damn smug about my master scheduling skills. I was learning how to play the game, and I had to say it felt really good to *have* a plan. For the first time since she'd reappeared back into my life, I knew what I was going to do.

I checked my watch.

Barely three hours.

Three more hours until I had her alone in a room with me.

This time?   There weren't going to be *any* interruptions.

21

By the time I made it back to my switchboard, I was a shaking mess of confusion, and worry, and hormones. A stop at the loo to put myself back in order hadn't helped much. I knew enough to realize I was in deep, serious trouble, but then, I also didn't have any earthly idea about how to get out of it either.

Neil wanted to fuck me. In his office.

And I would have let him.

What in the hell had gotten into Neil? Caveman plus Greek god equaled big problems for me. If Ethan hadn't interrupted we would've been going at it hard on his desk at that moment. Jesus Christ…

I sat there for a minute and tried to process what had just happened with Neil in his office.

What did all this mean coming from him? Was he trying to torture me?

Did he just expect I would sleep with him whenever the urge struck? Was that payback just then for leaving him all those years ago? Was he just being a manipulative bastard and trying to guilt me back into his bed because he thought he might get away with it?

Well, if so, then he was a delusional bastard as well as a manipulative one. I sat and seethed in my chair, getting angrier and angrier with every moment that passed.

I opened up my email and started typing.

TO: nmcmanus@bsiltd.co.uk
If you think I'm allowing you to drive me home tonight you are bloody dreaming! LEAVE ME ALONE!!!

I had some hope he really *got* my message, both literally and figuratively, because this time he didn't reply. Maybe some sense had been smacked into that thick head of his when the boss caught him trying to have sex with an employee on work premises. Wasn't my fault. This one was completely on Neil. He made the massive mess. He could sort it out.

Once five o'clock rolled around, I'd calmed down enough to think about my self-defense class. Maybe I'd learn some techniques I could use on Neil if he tried to seduce me in his office again.

Would there be a next time? *There can't be a next time, stupid.*

I told myself to shelve the matter for the time being, as I had to focus my attentions on the class I was about to attend. I left the locker room adjacent to the training facility dressed and ready. The memo had suggested comfortable clothes and shoes for the class, so I'd brought a bag along with me today with trainers and workout gear.

I came out into the main room where I was supposed to meet the instructor, someone named Terrence. The classes were one-on-one, to maximize the benefit of the time allocated. Apparently BSI didn't mess about when it came to this stuff.

The lights were on, and there was a PowerPoint set up in the back, but I didn't see anyone in the room.

"Hello?" I called out but was met with silence.

I walked over to the mat in the center and looked around the room. Typical workout facility with weight machines and treadmills, free weights and assorted equipment for training in the martial arts. Probably did the whole Krav Maga thing here, too. It was quite the rage and I had friends that never missed a class.

I'd keep an open mind, but I wasn't into that sort of thing really. I preferred taking walks outside, or maybe Pilates, or yoga in the park. I was into more mellow forms of exercise than what could be had indoors behind the walls of a gym.

I heard the sounds of the double doors opening behind me and turned to see.

Not my anonymous instructor named Terrence.

Neil.

Dressed all in black, nylon joggers and a long-sleeved dri-FIT that followed the form of his chest and arms like a second skin.

He walked slowly towards me; his eyes predatory again as they devoured my whole body.

Oh please, no!

"There's been a change of instructors. I'm afraid you get me."

Fuck.

"What the h-hell?" she stammered, her expression one of furious beauty, as well as utter contempt.

That's right. She can use it to her advantage.

"You cannot be serious," she said, her mouth falling open in surprise.

"Oh, I'm very serious about self-defense training for all employees at BSI."

"That's not what I meant, Neil, and you're very aware of it." She stomped her foot and pursed her lips together in a sexy pout that sent my cock into instant hardness. I wanted to kiss those angry lips of hers until she yielded to the inevitable.

Me, her—gettin' down to it. Once I cracked that hard outer shell she'd encased herself in, I'd have a way to reach her, and we could figure out the rest.

I shrugged at her and asked, "Shall we begin?" I held out my arm with the palm up, directing to a position on the mat where she should stand.

"No!" she shouted. "We're not beginning anything."

"You are here for a required class, yes?" I started pacing her, slowly in a circle. She turned her body to follow me. "You must be trained in self-defense." I pointed both fingers at her. "I'm here to teach you." I pointed my thumbs back at my chest, all the while still circling her, making her more and more uncomfortable as the seconds passed.

It's always good to have a plan.

"But you can't just come in here and be my instructor after what—what just happened in your office but three hours ago!"

"I don't see any other instructors in the room, do you?" I looked around at the walls for dramatic effect.

"Just me." I tightened my circle, getting closer in distance, and watched her eyes grow dark. My taunts were making her angrier by the second.

"This isn't right, Neil—f-for you to be doing th-this to me," she sputtered.

"There you go again with that word, Cherry. *This* is such a nebulous term in my opinion. I really think I need to demand a solid definition for your usage of the word *this*."

"Why are you being so cruel? Haven't I suffered enough, you sadistic arsehole!"

"Did it make you angry, Cherry? Do you want to beat me right now for what I tried to do to you earlier in my office?"

She glared and panted in short breaths, her beautiful breasts heaving under that tight pink sports top she wore. I desperately wanted to tear it off her and see her naked tits.

Soon.

I kept at her. "I would have you know, if E hadn't come in when he did?" I held my hands out in show of surrender. "Well, you know I would've had you spread out on my desk and screaming my name in under two minutes—"

She slapped me hard right across the face, the sharp sting bolstering me to finish the task at hand.

"Shut up! Shut your dirty mouth, you bastard. Why

are you saying such things to me? Why are you taunting me so cruelly?"

I held out my hands, offering my body, offering myself to her.

"That's right, Cherry, let it all out. Hit me. I can take it. Say what it is that's made you so very, very angry with me. It is me, isn't it? It's *me* that you're angry at."

She paused, breasts still heaving, her fury on the verge of release when I let her have the rest.

"Time for the truth now, beautiful girl. Come on!" I gestured toward my chest harshly. "No more lies, no more fading away into the background and giving up. Truth only. Say it out loud so I can hear you! SAY THE FUCKIN' TRUTH TO ME NOW!"

She hit me over the chest, arms and face, with all the wrath of a volatile female, enraged, and fighting her way closer to me with every smack and slap she dealt out.

"You didn't come for me. You should have come for me in Italy, and told me the goddamn truth. You let me believe in something that kept us apart. I loved you, and you let me stay away when you could have come to me! *YOU* DID THAT TO US, NEIL!"

She collapsed against my body then, crying in great anguished sobs, the fight gone out of her, the truth finally revealed.

I held her close and cradled her head against my chest; against my heart where she had always been, even when we were apart. Where she would always be.

"I know," I said against her ear, so she could hear me clearly. "I did that."

I took her face in my hands and lifted it up. My Cherry's face was wrecked with tears, and streaked with black eye makeup, and yet, the quiet stillness of her as I held her there to me, made her appear so beautiful. It was the truth of the moment I suppose. We were finally there on the same page, at the same time, reading the same fuckin' book.

"I know, I know, I know. I was wrong. I *should* have come for you." My thumbs caressed her cheeks as I held her, trying to make her understand. "I am so sorry."

I kept her face very close, held in my hands and brought my lips to hers.

She flinched.

"Let me, Cherry. Let me in now," I whispered softly, my plea both a request and a command.

I tried again, and this time she accepted my kiss. Her soft lips quivering under mine in beautiful acquiescence. I deepened the kiss. I showed her all we'd missed in the intervening years. I showed her how good it could feel to have your lover's tongue in your mouth. I showed her my love.

From there, things got crazy, to the point I was supremely grateful for disabling the video surveillance for this room.

I walked us to a padded wall and set her back up against it. Nothing was going to stop me this time. Nothing.

Not even her.

Neil's hands were all over me; his tongue was in my mouth, his body swallowing me up. I couldn't do much more than let him take me.

I was on fire, everywhere, and my mind was lost in the taste and the scent of him as we consumed each other in the training facility room, up against a upholstered wall.

He jerked up my sports top and growled when my breasts spilled out. It was a sound of hunger and raw emotion as he looked at me. My nipples were already hard, aching to feel his mouth on them again.

I threw my head back into the wall in ecstasy, when I felt that first exquisite touch of his tongue tasting my skin. He sucked, and bit, and licked at my nipples, and made me delirious with need. I held the back of his head to my breasts as he worked them over.

"I need you now," he said on a harsh breath.

"Yes…" Nearly incoherent with desire, I didn't care we were in a public room. Didn't care. Didn't think about anything beyond Neil and being as close together as we could get.

He'd already pulled away and dropped down to his knees. His hands went up to the waistband of my yoga pants and yanked them down. Hard. Knickers came with. He put his lips on the mound of my pussy and kissed softly, as if he were giving it a sweet greeting after so long being parted.

Well, it felt like it. My body knew his as intimately as was possible to know, and yet, here we were together in a brand new reality.

"Lift your foot," he said, before dragging my right leg free from knickers and yoga pants in one fell swoop. He left the other leg alone. We only needed one side unrestricted to accomplish the goal here.

Neil was back on his feet and kissing me before I could hardly take a breath, his hand sliding up my hip and over to the front, covering my mound with his whole hand.

"I want you, Cherry." He slid two fingers in between the lips. "Right here, right now." His fingers kept probing me, going deeper through the slick wetness he'd created, to find my clit.

I cried out when he made contact, the burn so good I knew he'd make me orgasm in another minute. He plundered my mouth with his tongue and my pussy with his fingers, sliding back and forth over my clit until I couldn't help but shout when the climax hit. His mouth over mine muffled the volume of my cries, as I rode it out on his talented fingers.

I felt him working the front of his joggers with his other hand, getting his cock out and ready for me.

"Here we go, beautiful girl," he said into my eyes, as he lifted my legs off the ground and opened me up. I felt the head of his cock kiss my entrance an instant before he buried himself deep inside me. "Fuuuuck," he moaned, "you're tight around me."

"Oh, God…" We both paused as we slipped into place together for the first time in many years. The awareness of what was happening between us, overwhelming. I let my thoughts drift as I clung to his strong arms. My back shifted into the soft wall over and over as the deliciously huge length of him stretched me decadently. In and out. Faster and harder we worked at it, our mouths glued together, our bodies struggling for the peak until I got there first, my inner walls clamping down reflexively around his cock.

I cried out as it happened, again, unable to move anymore, only capable of taking what he continued to give me.

Neil's eyes burned into me as he started to come, his penis growing harder and fuller as it jerked and swelled in the peak of his own orgasm.

Time slowed and mellowed, our foreheads pressed together, Neil still gently rocking into me, but now in the way of a caress. He kissed me softly, lovingly. It all felt very beautiful and right, but as my body came down from the high of the sex, reality dawned about what we had just done together.

"I'm going to put you down, okay?"

I nodded, the lingering pleasure being replaced by worry.

He pulled out of me carefully and set my legs down to the floor, steadying me until I had my balance. I felt so much wetness this time. I realized it was more than I'd ever felt before, just as I looked down upon a stream of shiny semen rolling down my thigh.

"Oh no...you didn't have a condom." I bent down to the floor and frantically tried to thread my foot back into the open leg of my knickers and tangled yoga pants, in a complete panic about what Neil would think, or say.

I pulled them on and my top back down to where I was decent and thought about running out the door. I really did.

Neil must have made an accurate assessment of my emotional state because he grabbed me by the upper arms and held me firmly to him. "It's okay. *Everything* is okay."

"But—but we didn't use—but you came insi—"

Neil kissed me on the lips, probably to shut me up more than anything, but it did help a little. "It doesn't matter," he said as he shook his head slowly back and forth, "because I don't care about condoms anymore with you."

I started to cry, all the emotion was just too much, and I needed some privacy. "I—I need to get myself cleaned up and d-dressed to go h-home."

"Shh, don't be scared. It's okay, Cherry. I'll help you." He kept running his hand over my hair as he soothed me with reassuring words.

"Neil?"

"I know a place. Come with me." He held my hand and wouldn't let go. Not one time did he release my hand as we took the lift back up to the forty-fourth floor, or later when he snuck us through a back entryway, that led to a locked door, which opened into a private suite behind his office. "This is mine and nobody else has access but me."

"I can take a shower?" I asked, now very unsure about everything and everyone. Even myself.

"Of course." He still had my hand in his and brought both of our hands up to his lips and pressed them in a soft kiss to the back of mine.

"What happens now, Ne—"

He kissed me firmly on the mouth, a demanding kiss of entitlement, his tongue pressing forward to find mine, moving in deep swirls. He finished in his own time, the intent to take charge of the situation very clear in his method.

"I'm keeping you here."

"What?" I asked him, my arms now clasped around his neck, holding on to keep my legs from buckling and sending me to the floor.

He smiled at me and found my lips again for another kiss, this one sweet, and gentle, and slow.

My worry felt less but my legs didn't feel even the slightest bit stronger.

"You're staying with me. Tonight…in this suite."

22

I knocked. "Elaina? Is everything all right?"

Nothing but the sound of the shower running returned to me.

Her silence worried me a little. The explosive nature of our reunion only verified how much of a struggle she was having with our training-room shag, and all of the emotions attached to it. Hell, I was dealing with more emotions than I cared to, myself. But more importantly, I didn't want her thinking too much.

Overthinking things was often the path to doom. We were both guilty of that one.

No, I wanted my Cherry Girl alone and private just as we were, dependent upon me to show her the way back...to the idea of us.

My plan was still intact.

I knew what she needed, and I would make sure she got every little bit of it.

I tried the doorknob after a minute and surprisingly, it opened. I stepped into the steamy air of the bathroom. There she was just sitting in the shower, her back up against the wall and her arms wrapped around her knees. She looked lost, biting down on her bottom lip by pulling the whole thing under her teeth. I wanted to suck and nibble on that bottom lip until she was breathless and not thinking about things that scared her anymore.

My beautiful girl needed *me* right now. She was also gloriously wet and naked.

I didn't say anything, just stripped down to my skin.

Naked was the way to play this. There would be no boundaries between us then. And keeping her naked would keep her in the room with me. She couldn't run away if she didn't have anything to wear. I had some intelligence, after all.

Her eyes flipped up to watch me as I undressed. And then, they widened when my shirt came off. That was the moment I knew. I knew that she saw it.

I stepped in and sat down opposite her on the shower floor. Face to face, body to body, hot water falling between us, droplets from the spray bouncing everywhere, coating our skin and hair. Wetting us both.

Elaina reached out her hand and touched my tattoo

with trembling fingers. "You got this to remember us?" she whispered in awe.

"I did."

"It is beautiful," she whispered again, as she traced the design with a fingertip, studying the ink carefully. "A dragonfly in the cherry blossoms…"

"Beautiful like you."

"Why did you have it done?—You got it…p-put on after I was…gone?" Even with all the water falling around us, I could see the tears pooling in her eyes as she asked the questions.

"Because I never stopped loving you and knew I never would. I wanted you forever in my skin."

A sob came up from out of her throat in a burst of air. She closed those glassy dark blue eyes of hers, and her whole body softened in what looked like great relief.

"So did I," she said softly, her eyes still closed and her lips still quivering.

Then she turned her back to me slowly, her head tilted to the side, extending her elegant neck. She reached around and pulled her wet hair off to the left, leaving her right shoulder exposed. As I gazed at her perfect skin, I almost stopped breathing when I saw the most stunning tattoo of cherry blossoms and branches done in sky blue and pink. It was very Asian in design and exotically inked, and also larger than I would expect for her slim body. Elaina didn't have any other tattoos, so for her to have such an impressive image placed permanently on her back, was a gesture of how meaningful our relationship was to her.

Fate can be beautiful and this is an example of one of those times. Don't ever forget this moment...or the gift of it.

My heart skipped a beat or two as I stared. I'd forgotten about what Ian had told me—his cryptic drunken comment about me not being the only one to have a cherry blossom tattoo. I'd been so focused on the events playing out between us, that it had slipped my mind. She'd never worn any clothes that would allow it to show.

"I wanted you forever in my skin too, Neil."

I traced the air above the design with my finger, just the tiniest little bit above the skin so I wouldn't wake her. *I wanted you forever in my skin too, Neil.*

My Cherry was in bed with me and she was asleep. I didn't want to disturb her but that didn't stop me from looking and enjoying.

She lay on her side—her body stretched out like a Greek goddess on a dais—the sheet partially draping over her body, but showing enough skin to make me want her again.

The wanting would never be a problem for me. I only had to think about her naked and I was ready. I'd had so many years of practice doing that, you see. Too fuckin' many.

I vowed I would never be in that situation again with her, though. Aching for her when she was lost to me. Afraid of trusting in the only person that could make it *right* for my heart. So much wasted potential. Wasted time.

"What are you thinking about?" she asked in a sleepy voice.

"You're awake, Cherry Girl?"

She rolled back over to face me, placing her two hands under her cheek on the pillow. "I am."

Her eyes moved over my face, studying me with the contented expression of a satisfied female. She looked happy again. She looked peaceful.

She had the look of a woman who was staying with me.

An expression I would have killed to have seen, if only for just one time, in the last six years.

"I was thinking about how beautiful a sight it is to have you naked in my bed. To have you close enough, where I can reach out and touch your warmth just like this."

I brought my hand to one of her breasts and caressed its softness, plumping the swell first and then ending with my fingers, drawing on her nipple, making it harden.

She gave me a sexy purr and a half smile.

"To smell the scent of you and me, after we've been making love together."

I buried my nose at her chest and drew it up, inhaling the unmistakable smell of sex, mixed with her intoxicating scent.

She arched her body closer and breathed a little heavier. My words and deeds were getting her hot.

"To taste the sweet flavor of you."

I covered her whole mouth with mine and plunged my tongue inside for a thorough taste, while my fingers found their way into her pussy lips for a slippery welcome. I pulled my hand back and popped those three fingers into my mouth, sucking everything off in a decadent show.

Another sexy moan as her eyes flared wide. Yep, she was gettin' hot for more.

"To show you just how much I love you, and that I can never bear to be without any part of you, ever again."

She looked down at our bodies under the sheets, seeing how hard my cock was, yet again, how much desire I had for her.

"I'm thinking about how I'm the luckiest fuckin' bastard on the planet because you're here with me."

I rolled her onto her back, splitting her legs very

wide with my hands behind her knees, making her calves rest on my arms. I sank my hips down into all that heaven of hers to find my center target. My cock aligned perfectly against her pussy, and I loved the flare of her eyes—the breathy sound from her throat—that intimate contact brought out in her as our parts touched.

She wanted more from me and my lad, and that was pretty much all I needed to know. Lad was willing, ready and able. Time to let him go again.

We'd been shagging determinedly since she showed me her tattoo in the shower. Making love so many times, I couldn't imagine why she wasn't sick of me already. Not a condom in sight. Felt too good going bare inside her to even consider. I hoped she didn't mind if we had lots of kids, because I'd never wrap up again with her.

But, by some miracle, she wasn't sick of me, because her eyes didn't lie. She had the look I remembered from long ago.

My beautiful girl was perfect in every way, and she showed me just how perfect by welcoming me every time. Every fuckin' time. And it was so good. So good it belied words for expression.

How blessed was I.

"And I can do this," I murmured roughly, finding her hands with mine and bringing them up over her head, pinning her underneath me, preparing her body to take me in.

She gasped in a breath, her eyes flaring at me in

submissive passion, her lips parting on the gasp.

I plunged in deeply—as far as I could go—the swift, sweet burn of her tight inner muscles clenching around my cock, in a sensation of pleasure so intense, it pulled a shout from me.

"Ahh, yes!" she cried, accepting the quick harsh thrust, and curling her fingers into mine where they intertwined.

I was lost. We could do this over and over and each time it felt better, more intimate, more effortless in the way we moved together, greater perfection in the way she accepted me.

We went slower, at a more leisurely pace, but no less intense than the other times. Making love to Elaina was not something to be rushed after all. I would always want to make it last.

I held her arms up with one hand and filled her with as much of me as I could manage. Cock, tongue, the fingers of my other hand. Whatever I could lick, penetrate, suck, or touch on her body, but still keep the pace.

I wanted another explosive climax out of her. I wanted to see the orgasm on her face when it happened. I wanted to feel the convulsive grip around my cock, and to hear the words she used to shout at me when she came.

The words.

I wanted the words from my Cherry, again.

Words that meant everything to me in regards to us.

Our rhythm increased, long slick slides of coming together, then moving apart before colliding into each other again and again and again.

I helped her along by circling her swollen clit with two fingers.

"I'm—I'm...c-c-coming," she moaned with the softest whisper, "Neil..."

Such a beautiful sound and so fuckin' sexy, it made me start to go off. My balls tightened up the instant she told me, rendering me a slave to her sweet cunt wrapped so tightly around my swelling cock.

Say it, Cherry. Say the words to me.

I kept going, riding her harder...faster...deeper.

She started to shudder and shake. Her mouth opened in an O and her head fell back, pushing out her breasts in a beautiful arch.

Say it!

I could feel the contractions of her walls gripping, and the burn down low, right before the spunk shot up the shaft.

Fuckin' say it, beautiful girl! I was gonna die if I didn't hear the words from her.

"I love you!" she cried.

"Again," I returned, still pounding into her hard.

"I love you so much, Neil."

I shattered.

There is no other word to express my experience in that moment. The orgasm shattered me. Elaina's declaration shattered me. My love for Elaina, and her acceptance of that love, shattered me. My Elaina loving me back, shattered me.

We crystalized together in a volcanic culmination of intimacy and pleasure that could only be felt. No description possible.

Minutes later we were still panting. Bodies still joined, hearts still pounding, separated only by the skin and bone that encased them.

"I see something worrying you on that beautiful face of yours." I traced her brow and then moved down her jaw, and finally to her lips, which were puffy and red from what I'd been doing to them for hours. "What is it?"

"You have to drive me home soon." She yawned sleepily.

Umm…I have you naked in my bed. Do you think I am fuckin' stupid, beautiful girl? I couldn't help the grin that spread over my face. "Well, I think you must have forgotten something you said to me earlier then."

"I'm sure I said a great deal of things to you earlier."

"You did. Things like 'yeeees', 'don't stop', and 'give me more of your big cock, baby.'"

She poked me in the ribs and tried to get in a tickle but I grabbed her hand, knowing I was in for a lifetime of sneak attacks seeing how she knew my secret.

"You pompous idiot, I did not say that," she laughed.

"But this one I have in writing, Cherry. You sent me an email at precisely 2:58 pm that said, and I quote, 'if you think I'm allowing you to drive me home tonight you are dreaming.'"

She smiled as understanding dawned and shook her head at me. "You still haven't worked it out quite right, mister. What I actually said was that you were 'bloody' dreaming."

I couldn't resist a kiss and gettin' in a good handful of her perfect arse cheeks, pulling her against my hips so she could feel what her body did to mine.

"Ahh, right you are. So in deference to your earlier wishes, I'm going to have to turn you down now, on taking you home."

"Hmm…well, you are a very conflicted person then, aren't you?" She raised a brow and clucked at me.

"No. Not at all. Why do you say that?"

"I seem to remember that I told you to 'leave me alone' as well, and you certainly ignored that request." She pointed her eyes down below my waist where my cock was half-hard again. "Obviously."

She laughed out loud, the sound of her laugh, making me so happy. Hearing the easiness in her, knowing we could amuse each other with silly idiotic comments and teasing, was indescribable.

"I love you," I said.

"I love you," she said.

"But I'm still not taking you home."

She frowned at me and pulled her lip into a pout. "I have no clothes for work in the morning."

"Where are your clothes from today?"

"I suppose they're still in my bag in the ladies locker room down at the training facility, where you seduced me."

I chuckled, realizing her sharp wit was going to give me lots of enjoyment from here on out. "You want me to go down there and get your bag for you?"

The warm feelings of amusement died a quick death when she glared at me like I had all of the intelligence of an earthworm. "I can't wear the same clothes to work as yesterday. People will know." Apparently, I had a great deal to learn about ladies clothing etiquette. She shook her head at me and yawned again, covering her mouth with the back of her hand.

I pulled her close, pressed my lips to her hair, and stroked down the long silky length of it with my fingers. I loved touching her cherry hair, and gratefully, she already knew that about me, and had never minded my obsession. "I'll take care of it. Go to sleep now, Cherry."

She was soft and pliable in my arms, snuggling in and getting comfortable for sleep when I heard her tell me again in a drowsy voice. "I love you."

The sweetest words.

The alarm on my mobile woke me. It took me a moment to figure out exactly where I was, but the soreness of my body reminded me as soon as I stretched. I looked around the *en suite* he had secreted back behind his office. Was this one of those bachelor pads used for meaningless sex? I had to admit, it didn't fit Neil's style from what I remembered, and yet, as I studied the pristine condition of everything from bed sheets to wall art, the place didn't appear to be used very often, either.

Where was he, anyway?

Regardless of wherever Neil was, I had to shower as soon as possible and dress in my workout gear so I could hop on the train for home. I couldn't very well show up to my workstation in what I'd worn the previous day, and I certainly couldn't wear trainers and sports bra with my skirt from yesterday either. I needed appropriate clothes to work in, and even though it would make me late to go home and get them, it couldn't be helped. I looked at the time again and bolted for the shower.

Washing my body in Neil's shower was almost something I didn't want to do. In a way, I was washing him away. So much sex last night. He'd made good on what he'd said to me in his office yesterday… *I want you in my bed so we can fuck all night long…over and over until you're a slave to it—just as you used to be.*

He'd gotten his wish. I *was* a slave to it again. And we had.

I hurried in the shower, becoming more nervous about the time.

When I stepped back out in the bedroom I saw there had been a sneaky delivery.

The bed was made and laid out upon it was my Burberry wool dress, brown on the top with a black skirt, boots, and my blue plaid overnight bag. I checked the bag and found my brush and hairdryer, makeup kit, knickers, bra, perfume, tights…everything I needed to prepare myself for the work day. Amazing.

He really was good.

I saw a note poking out from under the bag.

Cherry,

Thank you for staying. For that precious gift you gave to me. I can't ever take back what I said to you last night. It'll never change for me. The evidence is inked onto my skin forever. And onto yours, too. I love you, beautiful girl.

xo N

P.S. I snuck out and got some things from your mum so you can get ready for work. I'm stealth that way and she loves me tons, plus she always answers my texts. (don't be jealous)

P.P.S. If you're wondering where I am, it's down in the training facility [where I seduced you] having a work out. I need to keep strong so I can continue to take care of you as a good man should. XOX

I pulled his letter to my chest and held it there. And cried for how happy my man had made my heart.

23

"Please tell me it's safe to come in this time." E stuck his head in through the door *after* he rapped on it. "Are we behaving today? And more importantly, do I need to secure some legal representation—you know, somebody specializing in sexual harassment in the workplace?"

I looked at him and gave him my best deadpan expression, letting him continue on with his spiel, as he seemed to be enjoying himself immensely.

"Although, you must realize it will be a bit tricky as legal just happens to be *related* to the woman you've been trying to shag at the workplace." He mimed a grimace. "Sounds pretty bad, like you're going down, mate."

He stood there flapping his gob happily in the doorway, until I couldn't listen to him for another second.

"All right, are you done yet?"

E came in and sat in one of my chairs. "Do you mind?" he asked, gesturing to his shirt pocket where he kept the smokes.

"It's fine," I said, watching him light up and take a drag.

He grinned at me. "Well, I'm waiting."

"And you can keep on waiting, too, because I'm not talking."

E cocked one brow at me. "You christened the *en suite* too? Impressive, bro. When you jump, you really go in at the deep end."

"Piss off," I told him. "How in the goddamn hell do you know that? Those suites aren't monitored." He'd been harassing me for years about why I never used the *en suite* the way he used his. I'd always told him it was a waste of money on me because I'd never take a woman there. Now, he'd made me a liar.

He laughed. "I saw Elaina coming out of yours, looking very...hmm...how to describe her overall demeanor..." He tapped two fingers to the side of his head. "I know! She looked very...satisifi—"

"—Enough! You been taking fuckin' acting lessons there, E? Better not hold out for a career in film though, because you'd suck at it. Stick with your day job, please."

He ignored me and kept flapping on. "Come to think of it, you look a little more relaxed yourself. Like you've worked some of the edge off. Was the bed comfortable in there?"

"You can stop now. Please stop before I have to shut you up. And, it will look very bad if I have to go to the brig for killing the boss, which nearly happened yesterday, by the way."

He laughed some more, shaking his head, but then he gave me a genuine smile, something he didn't do very often. "I'm glad for you. I really am. She's lovely and you both deserve this."

"Thanks." I sighed deeply. "Six years is a long time to wait for someone. But we've worked everything out now, and...well, I'm just not letting her out of my sight again."

He nodded thoughtfully, losing the teasing tone and becoming serious as he smoked his clove cigarette in my office. "Six years...yeah, that is a long time." I could imagine where his mind may have taken him in the moment. Poor bastard had been through the worst kind of hell and survived it intact, when most men would have ended the pain and taken the easy way out. Lots of veterans came back with demons and did just that. His experience in the war amounted to the very worst there was, but yet, Captain Blackstone still had bollocks of steel, and the Victoria Cross to prove it.

"You love her." He didn't ask, but simply made a statement.

"Completely."

"Ahh." After another moment of reflection he asked, "How did you know you loved Elaina?"

"It's not something you have to figure out, E. The decision is made for you. When the right girl comes along…you'll already know."

He shook his head in dismissal as if he couldn't imagine such a thing ever happening to him. Lots of women had tried their best to catch him. I'd witnessed it for years, but I'd never seen him even look at any of them beyond a shag or two. Everyone knew Blackstone did not do repeat business with pussy.

I remembered to ask him why he'd come to find me. "Hey, what were you on about yesterday when you busted in here, anyway? You never said what was so important."

His expression changed again. This time to one of pride. "Guess which firm got tapped to secure the RF at the Games?"

"Her Majesty?" I couldn't help bolting up out of my chair in excitement for what this meant for BSI. This was bloody huge.

"Yeah. They asked us to do it." Ethan was grinning from ear to ear.

TO: emorrison@bsiltd.co.uk
How did you like your breakfast? xo N

Since Elaina ran the switchboard, texts on her mobile were hard for her to manage. So were calls, so our best mode of communication was going to be email when at the office. Oh, I could still see her at her station via the bank of security cameras that played out doings all over the floors housing Blackstone Security International, but the most important one for me would always be reception area on the executive level, forty-four. I had Elaina programmed to display on the biggest monitor in my office.

She didn't care for me spying, so I didn't advertise the fact to her, but I sure loved to be able to look up and see her while I was at my desk working. It just made me happy to be able to see what she was doing, who came into the offices, watching her move around and talk to people. I'd been starved for so long, it was painful to have to look away sometimes.

TO: nmcmanus@bsiltd.co.uk
I loved the cherry scone, but I loved my clothes most of all. Thank you for the note too. You made me have tears. P.S. Good ones   xxE

Her sassy comebacks made me smile, and made me hard. I would have gone out to reception and picked her up, carried her back to bed and made love to her again, if I could have gotten away with it.

TO: emorrison@bsiltd.co.uk
I have an important question to ask you. xo N

I knew she would hit me with something snarky and hilarious right back. That was the fun part. Anticipating what she would say, and knowing it would be a surprise anyway.

TO: nmcmanus@bsiltd.co.uk
Well mister, you should know that I always say 'no' first, to anything and everything, as a general rule. xxE
P.S. You should also know that it is not at all pleasant to have to imagine the texts that went back and forth between my mother and my man last night. Bleh.

Christ, if she only knew how many times I'd stopped by her house to help her mum when she was still away in Europe. If Ian had been off on a business trip somewhere, their mum would ring me and ask for help. And I was always happy to stop by and help the woman who'd welcomed me as a son from the very first time we'd met. But, what nobody ever knew about was how I would go into Elaina's bedroom and look around. Sometimes, I'd touched her things, even smelled them, to see if I could find any trace of her still left behind. I didn't like remembering that part, but felt that it was too important of an experience to ever forget. If I remembered how much we'd lost, then it would help me to make sure it never happened again.

I still had more of my plan to put into action, and wouldn't stop until it was fully executed.

TO: emorrison@bsiltd.co.uk
You're going to want to say 'yes' to this one. Trust me. As for the texts between your mum and me? Don't think about them. See? No problem whatsoever. Easy. xo N

She got busy with some clients who came through, and it was a while before she could respond. I loved to listen to the sound of her voice speaking in Italian or French on the international calls, too. It was sexy as hell, and made me so proud of her for what she'd made of herself with no help from anyone, just her own initiative.

TO: nmcmanus@bsiltd.co.uk
I think you forgot to ask me the question, Captain. Focus, please. :P

I couldn't wait to get her to my place that night. First time. My real bed. Total privacy, and the luxury of knowing where in the hell she was and what she was doing for the whole night long. And, how she was getting to work the next morning (with me), and how she was getting from work back to my place again (with me). Huge fuckin' window, with a city lights view of London. Just thinking about it got my cock throbbing. My Cherry Girl and I had a date in front of that window coming to us.

TO: emorrison@bsiltd.co.uk
May I drive you home tonight, Cherry?

Her reply came back to me instantly.

TO: nmcmanus@bsiltd.co.uk
Yes you may. (I love it when you drive me) *blushing*

I checked the time and blew out a sigh. Five more hours. Five more hours before I could make good on my promise, and have my blushing girl right where I wanted her.

"When may I look?" I asked impatiently. "I want to see everything."

"In another moment. Almost there." Neil had a hold of my hand, leading me through his flat.

I kept my eyes closed, well…only because he told me to do it. One of the unspoken, but clearly understood quirks about us—an element of that made us work so well—was the way in which he was never indecisive with me. He always knew what he wanted, how to ask for it, demand it, get it, or if he must, how to take it. This combination of his large, commanding presence made the whole package of Neil a devastating elixir.

He liked to surprise me with little things and to spoil me. He'd helped me pack enough clothes to last through the next few days of work, without the panic of one of those weird nightmares where everyone has clothes on but you. Hate those.

After leaving my house and kissing Mum on the cheek, and thanking her for allowing him to take me away, he'd wined and dined me at *Gladstone's*, being the romantic, thoughtful man he'd always been, and still was. The wine, and the mouthwatering vision of him across the table, had left me a little intoxicated, and I knew I couldn't be in safer hands than his. But, at that moment, he had my scarf over my tightly closed eyes and was leading me along blind, to something inside his flat he wished to show me.

"Now?" I asked again.

He stopped us and moved behind me, placing me where he wanted me with his hands on my upper arms. Next, I felt the silk of my scarf being untied from the back of my head with his large fingers tugging gently on the fabric. I loved Neil's fingers. They worked a kind of magic on me. He touched me with them and I became a hot mess, desperate for him to do other things to me with more parts of his body.

My eyes were still closed.

"You can open them now, Cherry."

It took me a moment to utter any words.

"I—I can't believe how beautiful it is." The dark night was illuminated by the millions of fairy lights of London.

He stayed quiet.

"This is what you wanted to show me first?" I reached out a hand and touched the glass. "The view out the window." It was indeed, stunning. A whole wall of glass extending out over the city, both the old and the new, lit up and shining against the stark midnight-blue sky.

"Yes." I felt him step back and break contact with me.

I turned my head and saw he'd moved to a padded bolster cushion and sat down on it.

"Do you remember what I asked you to do for me the first time we made love at Hallborough?" he asked softly.

"You wanted me naked against the view in the window."

"Yes, that's right, Cherry. You do remember…"

"I do, Neil." I stretched my arms up behind my neck and dragged my palms up through my hair at the back of my scalp. "And now?"

I saw him swallow deeply and his eyes widen. I liked to hear his commands, so I waited for him to tell me. I loved the look on his face right then, too. Like a fierce golden beast waiting until the perfect moment to pounce upon his prey. I was the prey. *Lucky, lucky, me.*

"Strip for me in front of this window, Cherry. All the way down to your skin…so my London view is finally the way I've always needed it to look for me, in this house. This window—this view—you in front of it. Do that for me now."

I steadied my racing heart and slowly stripped for my man.

He watched me do it in silence, in stillness.

I imagined this was something more for him than

just a prelude to what was certain to be an orgasmic explosion at its conclusion. This was our second beginning.

Only his eyes followed my movements. They tracked my arms as I removed my dress and dropped it to the floor. They lingered on my legs as I unzipped my boots, then peeled off my tights. They glittered when my bra came off, and flashed when my knickers were released from my hand, to land silently somewhere on the heap of garments littering the furry rug beneath my feet.

He leaned back in his position on the bolster and looked at me some more, his elbows propping up his big body, legs stretched out in front of him, ankles crossed. He seemed in no hurry to rush me, but content to savor something he'd wanted for a long time.

I gave him as much time as he wanted, content to wait for the next request.

"Turn around, and look out at the view," he said on a breath.

I did it, totally confident in the knowledge that nobody but Neil would see me. The photographer in him had organized this, so there would be no backlighting. I knew my man well.

I heard the sounds of zippers and belts and clothes coming off. The thud of shoes and trousers being discarded, the clink of metal, as things were abandoned to wherever they happened to fall.

"Move your legs apart and put your palms forward on the frame of the glass."

A shiver rolled down my spine as I complied with his request. I waited for something to happen, becoming more aroused and needy by the second, when suddenly, I sensed him very close, although I'd not heard him moving toward me.

I could smell the spiced, clean scent of him, and I heard a long, controlled breath being released along my back.

Then…his tongue took a long, wide lick forward up the seam of my pussy.

I shouted through the contact, unable to muffle the cries of extreme pleasure as he devoured my sex with his mouth. I arched back to give him better access and gripped the window frame to keep myself upright.

He was relentless with his mouth. And his fingers— gripped my hips firmly, kneaded the flesh, and held me apart so he could continue to fuck me with his tongue, until he knew I was climaxing. Oh yes, he would know when it happened. His lips would feel me, and his tongue would taste me. Any second it would happen…

So when he pulled away, I nearly fell down to the floor and wept.

I must have made sounds of protest, because he growled at my ear, "I know, beautiful girl…I know."

Then his cock took the place where his tongue had just been.

We both shouted together as his enormous length burrowed all the way in, bumping the wall of my cervix with a sharp luxurious sting.

"I love you so much…" he moaned at my shoulder, as he reared back. And then he powered forward violently.

The pace was wicked, the thrusting fierce, the pleasure intense, as he found his rhythm with me. I floated away to a place where thinking was not possible, nor important. We both knew where we were and what we were doing.

It was finally right.

So very right…when Neil fucked me against the panoramic window of his flat, that looked out upon the city of London, in all her nighttime glory… So very right…when Neil claimed me for the second time in our lives.

He brushed his hand up and down my hip absently as if he didn't want me to forget he was there.

As if I could ever forget when he was touching me.

We were now spooning on our sides in front of the window, snuggled into the thick fur rug on the floor. The rug was so decadently soft, and although I appreciated its cushioning from the hard floor, I didn't need its warmth. I had my man right up against me to keep me warm. My body was burning with heat anyway, from what we'd just done together, and continued simmering for a good long while. I didn't feel like I could ever be cold again.

"Thank you," he whispered at the edge of my shoulder, pressing his lips there before moving them on to the next spot, little soft kisses on my skin in a trail up my shoulder to my neck.

"My pleasure," I purred.

"Yours *and* mine," he said.

"I've still not gotten a tour of your flat yet, you know."

"You've seen the only part that's ever really mattered to me, though."

"The window was that special to you, Neil?"

"Yes."

He was quiet for a moment and then he said, "You don't really need a tour anyway."

"Why don't I?"

"Because this is your home now. You live here."

I stiffened in shock. "I don't remember being asked such a thing."

He rolled me onto my back and leaned over me, his hand coming up to hold one side of my face. "Cherry, will you live here with me? Make this your home? With me?"

His chocolate eyes glittered down at me, his thumb brushing back and forth over my cheekbone. The love in his eyes answered every question I needed answering. I knew he loved me, as I loved him. I didn't really need him to ask me, because I knew I was home. Home *was* Neil. I wasn't the young girl he'd loved before, though. Long years had changed us both, but my answer was really, very easy, and simple.

"I love you…so yes," I answered him with a kiss to those precious lips of his that knew how to love me so well.

Neil got up first, then, bent down to pick me up from the rug, kissing me sweetly, as soon as he was on his feet. He smiled at me, and then he started walking, carrying me off somewhere, down the hallway of my new home.

I didn't care where, and could only imagine his intent was to show me the bedroom where I would be sleeping from that point on.

24

"Just like my brother to be out of the country when there's work to be done." Elaina was checking her text messages as I drove us to her mum's. "This is what he sent me: 'Sorry sis, off to Paris. Big clients with deep wallets have me shouting Vive la France! Scotty can do without my help just fine. He's bigger and stronger than me. –Ian.'" She scoffed at her mobile in disgust. "What an arse."

"True. But think about if he did help move you into my flat how we wouldn't be able to get rid of him after. He'd stay for hours and hours, drinking all my Guinness and expecting us to feed him."

"That's a very good point, Captain." She turned in the seat to face me as I drove, a frown marring the smoothness of her brow.

"What are you thinking about, Cherry Girl? I see those cogs in your pretty head churning something fierce."

"Well you should be keeping your eyes on the road and not the cogs in my head," she retorted, in that sassy way that made me want to do really filthy things, involving her pouty lips and my cock.

"You can tell me whatever it is, you know." I reached a hand over and found one of hers. "It's in my new job description. All part of being your man."

She pulled my hand up to her soft sweet lips and kissed my palm. "It's Mum. She's been drinking more in the last few days and I'm worried about why."

"Yeah, I noticed. And you think it's because you're moving out of her house?"

She shook her head. "Don't think so. I was away for years and she lived alone. I've only been back for a short while so she couldn't have gotten that dependent upon me in just a few weeks. Besides, her whole point of leading me back to London was to get us back together. She wants this for us. Why would it send her down now that her wish has happened?"

"I don't know. And you're right, it doesn't really make sense." Caroline Morrison's strength and devotion to me had sustained me for many years. Her love and support had never been questioned. In my head, she took over the role of mother that my gran had previously held. There wasn't anything I wouldn't do for her if she needed me. "Let's try to get her to come to the flat with us today. She can see where we're living with her own eyes and know she's wanted, and welcome to visit any time she likes. I'll take you both to dinner after we get your things sorted, and maybe we can do some detective tag teaming, and pull it out of her."

She sighed into the seat and gave me a half smile. "You are aware that when we chose to adopt you, we made out the better in the deal, aren't you?"

I shook my head. "No, darlin'. I am the luckiest man in the world. I believe that, and I never forget when I gained Ian as a friend, I gained not only a brother, but a whole family."

The minute we entered the house I knew something was off. It was far too quiet. Neil noticed, too. I could see it in how his body tensed, and in the way he moved quickly but methodically, going through the house for clues.

"Mum?" I called loudly.

Silence.

"She was expecting us. She knew we were coming at noon to pack up everything," I reasoned, now starting to really worry.

"Her car is here. Maybe she popped in to see a neighbour or something—" He paused, tilting his head up to the ceiling as if he'd heard a noise. He pointed up. "Your attic has the pull-down staircase doesn't it?"

"Yes, but why would she go up to the attic—"

A loud thump sounded right above us.

Neil was already up on the second floor and opening the latch that released the attic staircase to come down before I even made it half-way. He started climbing the ladder while it was still unfolding from the ceiling.

"Is she up there?" I asked impatiently.

I heard him say, "Oh, Mum, that's no good."

"I am fine, dear," Her voice sounded like my mother, but when I made it up the stairs and saw her for myself, she didn't look at all like my mother. She was very disordered, still wearing her robe, hair not brushed, definitely intoxicated and it was barely noon.

"Mum...what's happened?" I sat down beside her on the old chaise lounge and put my arm around her. "Did you sleep the whole night up here? It's freezing." I rubbed up and down her arm to get some circulation and warmth into her.

She held out a hand toward the room and then let it fall. "Oh, Elaina..." She turned her head away from me in shame and sobbed quietly. Boxes of my father's clothes, and mementos, were opened and strewn all about us, along with an empty bottle of Bombay Sapphire and Schweppes. The most significant item though, appeared to be what looked like a letter pressed to her breast.

I tried to make eye contact but she wouldn't look at me. She just continued to cry with her head turned away, with that paper clutched to her heart.

Neil crouched down to meet her at eye-level. "What's this, Mum?" He took hold of the corner of the paper. "May I read? Did something in this letter upset you?"

She allowed him to pull it from her hand.

"What does it say?" I demanded, knowing full well he hadn't had enough time to figure out what it was about.

Sometimes you just know when things are bad. The sense of dread cloaking me affirmed without a shadow of a doubt, that whatever the letter contained—it was something very ominous.

Neil's face went pale, and my heart skipped a beat as I continued to rub up and down Mum's arm.

"It's from the US Department of Defense in Washington D.C.." He looked at me with compassion in his beautiful dark eyes that loved me so well, and tried to soften the blow.

My hand flew up to my mouth in a gesture to brace myself. "Dad?"

"Yes. It says they've identified the remains of George Morrison through advanced DNA analysis. It is a request for the wishes of the family to be made known to them so…the final resting place for his bodily remains can be, um…resolved." Neil hated to say those words to us. I could tell it hurt him to speak them.

"Oh…Mum…" Nothing else would form on my lips. I was so stunned, trying to process what the letter was asking of us, and worried about the present state of my mother, I couldn't really come up with anything better. What was there to say? Dad was gone, as he'd been since 11, September, 2001. This certainly brought up so much of the feelings I'd put away deep, deep inside of me. They shot straight to the top of the emotional queue, all in a split second. I couldn't even imagine how Mum had been dealing with it…and that she'd kept it to herself and not told her children. Well, I could see how she dealt with it. By way of a bottle of Bombay.

And that scared the absolute shit out of me.

"Mum…when did you get the letter?" Neil asked gently.

She choked out another anguished sob and said, "It came a week ago Friday."

I was afraid to ask the next question, but knew I had to. I looked at Neil and gathered my courage, because I had a feeling about what she would say. "What do you want us to do, Mum?"

She snapped her head around to look at me, took my cheek in her hand and held it there. Tears streaming down her lined, but still beautiful face, she told me what she wanted.

"My darling, please—please go there and bring him back—bring Daddy back to his home—to the family that loves him. I cannot b-bear the thought of him being…th-there all alone…and so far away from us."

"Okay, Mum. I will go."

I answered my mother quickly because I already knew what she was going to ask me. Also, because there was no other answer I could've given to her. I would go to Washington D.C. to get my father and bring him home. No matter how hard this was going to hurt, I'd do what had to be done.

"And I'll be right there with her," Neil said, embracing both of us into his strong arms, that thankfully could bear the weight of two broken hearts.

The mortuary at Dover Air Force Base housed the remains for victims of the Pentagon crash on 9/11. I wondered how they'd handled the hundreds of families that had come through there, grieving for lost loved ones over the past decade. I mostly worried about how they were going to handle things with Elaina. I pulled her hand, clasped in mine, up to my lips as we walked down the hallway together.

"Okay?" I asked.

Her midnight-blue eyes blinked at me solemnly, and then she nodded. "I'm really glad you're here with me."

"Nothing could have kept me away. Wherever you go, so must I."

Elaina mouthed the words "love you" to me as we followed behind the servicewoman who was leading us.

She stopped us at a room that appeared to be set up, just as a viewing area in a funeral parlor would be. Darkened lighting, rich décor with stained-glass windows, and even a platform of sorts. This whole experience was eerie. The very idea that this facility had returned partial remains, so many times, to so many families—the Yanks had been forced to make a room especially for the purpose—was depressing. I worried about what Elaina would be presented with. It didn't take profound logic to understand that there wasn't going to be a body for George Morrison. If there had been a body for him, it would've been identified almost immediately, not a decade later. There would be very little for the family to claim, and I ached for my girl, and her mother, and brother over it.

"Right through here is where you'll take possession." Staff Sergeant Knowles gestured with her arm. "The documentation is on the altar beside your father's remains, and you'll take that with you as well." She gave instructions for Elaina and spoke to her directly. "This room is yours for however long you need it. When you'd like to leave, please use the exit out the hall and to the right. As you come out of the building, you'll see the car waiting to take you back to your hotel." She smiled placidly, as if she'd done her small speech thousands of times and could recite it in her sleep. "Whenever you're ready, though. Again, please take all the time you need."

Yes, Dover AFB had done this far too many times

258

for my liking. The Yanks had a protocol, which had been honed to perfection because of it. I hated the whole thing. I hated that George Morrison had been killed in a terrorist attack. I hated that a good man had been snuffed out needlessly, as so many others had been, in a pointless war, over semantics…and ideals that would never change any minds. Stupid.

My own service, in the very same war, had made me somewhat of a cynic. Seeing troops die right in front of me was something my mind probably would never let go of. Lost friends and brothers, people you talked to, ate meals with. People you trusted with your life. Lost. Taken. Dead. Was hard for me to evade feelings of guilt, when I still had a life, and they no longer did. Why them and not me?

I also hated that the daughter had to be here claiming the few small bits of her father, a decade after his death, so the family had something to bury. I hated what the circumstances of his death had done to Mum, to Ian, and to Elaina. It brought home the knowledge of how quickly somebody you loved could be taken away from you forever. Like Gran—like my own mother.

Sergeant Knowles gave a salute and left us, the sound of her boots in regulated step, tapping out a beat as she departed, leaving us in quiet once again.

Elaina started forward to the altar, still holding tightly to my hand. She hadn't broken down or been visibly upset by going there, but I knew it had to be very hard on her to be the one to actually make the trip. There was never a doubt in my mind about coming with her. She needed me and that was all. Family came first, no matter what. The Morrisons *were* my family.

We stopped at the altar and looked down at the two things placed there. An envelope and a small square box made of cardboard, with a self-closing lid and label marked with his name and address.

Elaina put her hand out and touched it. "It's so tiny…"

I didn't know what to say. I just put my arm around her and looked down at the small, tidy box containing some small portion of her dad.

A whole person reduced to what could fit inside a minute cardboard box.

"Let's go now," she said.

Elaina picked up the box and the envelope in her hands and looked up at me. Not much expression on her beautiful face, just a kind of blankness that showed me she was suffering from no small amount of shock. She had to be in disbelief at what she'd been given of her father to bring home.

"I want to leave this place."

So I walked her outside of the building and into the sunshine. A few puffy white clouds in a clear blue autumn sky displayed above our heads. We both looked up at it and I imagined we were both thinking the same thought that didn't need to be expressed out loud.

This day was very much like the final day of George Morrison's life.

I sat at the table in our hotel room and stared at the box. A box that held some small parts of my father inside it. So many emotions were boiling around inside my head. Things I'd put aside over the years because the passage of time does dull the ache when you have to live daily life. Also, I'd been a child when he'd died, so the more years that passed without him, made the time I'd had with my father become shorter by comparison. In a way, death is easier than letting go. When the person is gone, you have no choice but to accept that fact. Death is final. When they are still alive but lost to you, the grief stays alive, too.

But Mum had had many wonderful years with my dad. I thought about Neil, and how it would be for me if something like this happened to us. If he was just…gone. And there was never another chance to be together again. I shuddered. Yeah, G&T's every day didn't seem like something that far off the mark, when I put it in my terms. My mother had lost her husband, the father of her children, the love of her life. Who was I to judge how she handled her grief? I didn't even know how I would present this—what should I even call it?—portion of my dad to my mother, when we arrived back home.

"Neil, I can't bring him back to Mum in this…box. There has to be something better we can find."

His response was to bring his hand up to the back of

my neck and rub with his thumb gently back and forth. He'd been so good about everything, showing me, with his quiet strength and support, how much he loved me, and my family. I'd done a number on Neil when I'd left him six years ago. I realized now, how much my abandonment had hurt him to the point he was unreasonably worried about me going anywhere without him. I suppose he was still afraid I might not come back.

This was something I agonized over each time I saw the signs of his obsessive worry about me. It made me feel guilty and I didn't like feeling that way. I knew he had me on surveillance in his office at work, that he could watch me at my station and hear me talking to clients and such. I was being patient with him for now, but I didn't think it was healthy for us, either.

"I saw some shops on the street like antiques and even a pawn shop, I think. Maybe you can find something suitable in one of them. You want to go right now?" he asked.

"You don't have to come with me, you know." I sighed without meaning to. "I'll be fine by myself. It's just a block of shops on the same street as this hotel."

He shook his head at me and frowned. "I'm coming with—"

"You don't have to worry anymore, babe. I know I hurt you badly, and I own up to what I did to you by leaving like that." I put my hand on his face. "But I'll always come back to you. I love you and I can't live without you. There is nothing that will ever keep me from my man again. I'll always come back to you. Promise."

The look he gave me nearly split my heart in two. His eyes turned glassy and he brought his head to my lap and just rested it there, saying nothing. He reached for my hand and clasped it against his lips. I ran my fingers through his hair with my other hand and we just stayed like that for a while. No words needed. We communicated just fine without them.

Decisions were permanent, and although we could regret some of them, we couldn't call them back. I had made some poor ones. Neil had too. I guess the best we could hope for, was to love each other as honestly as possible on each day we had left together. And hope for many, many long years of those days in our future.

He still had his head in my lap when he asked, "I want to take you somewhere before we go back to London. Please?"

"Of course, my darling," I answered immediately. "Wherever you go, so must I."

25

From Washington D.C., Neil brought me to Scotland.

He told me he just wanted one weekend where we could rest and be together, without any distractions from work, or the myriad of other problems that had a way of taking one's attention away from what you really wanted to be doing. He needed me all to himself, according to him.

He'd also said, that it was time for me to see his inheritance from the uncle he'd never met.

The whole idea of it still amazed me. Neil, a landowner, and from the looks of it, there was *a lot* of land involved.

"I can't believe this," I mumbled looking from the window as the car pulled into a long drive bordered with more trees.

"What can't you believe, Cherry?" Neil was doing that thing where he liked to surprise me and gave virtually no information, just to torture me. Made me insane, but he sure seemed to be enjoying himself.

"This is a bloody estate with an enormous amount of land and, well, you made out like it was just an old house on a plot with some trees, not something out of *Pride and Prejudice*."

"Is that Mr. Darcy's house you mean?"

"Yes, it was named *Pemberley*, if you care to know." I still hadn't seen Neil's house come into view yet, and was getting very impatient as I peered out the window.

"I'll make a note of it." He leaned over to give me a kiss on the side of my temple. "I know how you love your romance books. You're always reading in bed."

"And you're always making a point to distract me when I'm *trying* to read in bed."

"Damn straight, woman. Do you think I'm a moron or something?" He nuzzled my neck.

"Shhh." I pointed stealthily in the direction of our cab driver with my finger.

"But I'm just kissing your neck," Neil whispered,

"that doesn't make any sound."

I continued looking out the window, and let out a scream about a minute later when our cab turned down what looked to be a private road.

"Who is needing a very firm "shhh" now, huh?"

I didn't pay any attention to him. My eyes were riveted to what framed the road. Lining both sides of us were trees completely covered with white and pink blossoms. A surprise for November, but they were definitely blooming. The Autumn Cherry. *It comes into bloom for a second time in autumn.* All the way up the drive leading to his house.

"These are the autumn cherry trees you told me about..."

"Yes, darlin'. Aren't they pretty?"

I didn't answer him. I couldn't because my vocal chords had frozen. I nodded my reply to him with my hand firmly attached to the window of the cab.

Rivers of tears were streaming down my face.

The next minutes were a blur as I indulged in an ugly-cry moment. Neil seemed to know what to do with me, though. Thankfully, he took charge of everything else in his life so competently, and, it seemed, me as well. He'd always had an uncanny ability to know when he needed to—the part about taking charge of me.

He paid the driver and sent him away, before leading me up the stone steps of his *house* on very wobbly feet.

Mansion was a much more accurate description of what I was staring at.

Four massive, white stone pillars held up the façade, which framed a beautiful door painted in a rich shade of dark blue. Yellow and grey stone, trimmed with white bricks made up the rest of it. The house was flanked by colossal pine and oak trees on a lush green park, one that spread out for what seemed like miles.

He then greeted an older man, with graying hair, who appeared to be waiting at the top of the steps for us. Neil introduced him to me as Batesman, and the two of them had a small chat, while my knees felt like they would buckle at any moment. I made a valiant attempt to say hello and not frighten the poor man to an early death. Highly doubtful I could be successful on that one. Well, we would just have to wait and see if Mr. Batesman died in his sleep tonight, wouldn't we? Wait, more importantly begged the question—Neil had a servant? In his Scottish mansion? On his frickin' country estate?!

My head suddenly ached terribly.

I needed a ginormous glass of red and then a chaser of something much stronger. This was Scotland; maybe there were bottles of hundred-year-old Scotch down in the cellars left over from the smuggling days of Jack Sparrow and his ilk. I'd bet my sarcastic thought was closer to the mark than not.

I followed along as he led me by the hand, and felt more and more out of my element. My sense of security with him, of us, felt strangely threatened. This was all something new to me. A part of him I had no knowledge of, introduced into his life at a time when I wasn't there. He'd learned everything of this place...without me.

I let him lead me along blindly, as I was no longer able to see anything of the inside of his magnificent house, my eyes so blurry with tears.

Neil knew what was going on with me, though. He always knew.

Without a word, he paused at the bottom of a huge staircase before scooping me up in his arms. He carried me up that marble staircase and brought me to a room with a four-poster bed made up with a plush white duvet.

He laid me back onto the soft, fluffy down cover and hovered over me, his eyes flickering over my face, reading me, understanding how hard it was to let go of regret. He must have regrets, too. I knew he had them, and that they were the reasons he forgave me for mine.

"I know what you need, Cherry," he told me, as he descended. "Let me take care of you."

His soft lips kissed, and his warm tongue licked away every tear on my face, until any sad thought that weighed upon my conscience was set aside for that moment. He stripped me out of my clothes slowly, piece by piece, until I was totally naked and he could trail his hands and mouth over me.

Until no part of my body was left untouched. Until

he'd given me too many orgasms to count. Until he'd made me feel reassured of my place with him, in Scotland. Yes, my man knew me well.

He left the bed and stripped out of his own clothes. Less slowly than he'd undressed me. He was ready for me, well before his trousers landed somewhere on the floor.

When he returned, I sat up and pushed my hands on his chest, forcing him back down into the softness of the bed. "My turn."

He smiled at me, his lips still glossy from what they'd been doing to me for the past glorious minutes, as realization dawned on his handsome face.

I got comfortable and took his thick cock in my hand, stroking up and down the velvet skin that sheathed the rock hardness underneath. I wrapped my mouth around the head of him and drew deeply, sucking to the back of my throat until I couldn't take him any farther.

"Oh, fuckin' fuck yes…" he growled, as I went to work on his beautiful penis.

And it was beautiful. Neil in the throes of passion was breathtaking to me. I wouldn't say no to a picture or two if he ever offered. Golden male beauty with muscles honed to perfection, tight and straining beneath me, because of what I did to him. From what I made him feel. With all the love I could give to him with my whole heart.

I sucked him to the brink, until I was waiting for his

release of semen to land in my mouth, when he pulled completely out of and away from me.

"No, I want—" he whispered harshly, before repositioning himself and lifting me under my arms. He hauled me back onto his lap, set me down onto his cock, and thrust inside me violently. He took control of his orgasm, as his mouth claimed mine, just as roughly as his cock had just claimed my sex. "Cherry, Cherry...Cherry—I love...YOU," he chanted against my lips.

His hands gripped at my hips almost painfully, keeping our bodies fused together, his cock buried deep inside me, even after he'd laid back into the softness of the bed, and brought me with him.

After we settled down from the rush, he pulled the duvet over us to keep off the autumn chill. I moved to rearrange my body but he gripped my bum and kept us connected. "Stay like this with me."

I touched his face and held it. "Why?"

"Because I want to be in you."

"Why?" I had my theories about what he was doing.

His eyes looked to the left, betraying his untruth. "I love being inside you after. I love you."

"I love you too, and I think I know what you're trying to accomplish." I rested my chin carefully on his sternum so I wouldn't hurt him. "It's probably not going to work though. You know I'm on the pill. You've seen me taking them."

He sighed slightly, his expression giving up in defeat, that I had routed out his motivation for coming inside me, instead of letting me take him in my mouth.

"Well, I hope they fail at some point, because you're the only woman who'll ever be mother to my kids."

When I admitted to my caveman plan to knock her up so I'd never lose her again, she smiled. My Cherry Girl knew me so well.

"You don't have to get me pregnant to keep me. I'll stay either way," she said sweetly, before resting her cheek to my chest.

I stroked up and down her back and pictured her and me with our future children. There should be a few, I thought. Boys and girls that looked like her, and never had to know a life without loving parents who were there every step of the way, helping them to grow, and become good people.

"I'll still work on it, thank you very much," I said. "I have a plan all sorted out, Cherry…and, as you've learned—" I coughed and muttered the words, "self-defense training classes" under my breath, "—I take my plans in regards to you *very* seriously."

She giggled and snaked her hand down to my ribs for a jab.

"Oh, that's gonna get you something for sure, beautiful girl," I said to her, as I rolled her beneath me.

I kept my promise.

Over and over again.

Six weeks later

"HAPPY NEW YEAR!" The unanimous cries of guests rose up, and then it got quiet as couples greeted each other with kisses to ring in the New Year. I didn't care about any others, though. Just one person held my attention.

And my heart.

The party had everybody in high spirits, because the announcement had been made about BSI gaining the contract to secure the Royals at the London Games next summer. And it was a momentous accomplishment for the business. But, I had something even more momentous on my mind for that moment. The focus of which had everything to do with my Cherry Girl, who looked mouthwatering as usual.

She wore a chocolate-brown lace dress that hugged her shape in a way that should probably be illegal. Her sky-blue shoes and jewelry, the colour she loved so much, contrasting beautifully. Her unique, cherry-colored hair, arranged on one side, fell in a long wrap of curvy waves. I'd have my hands buried deep into it later. When I got her home and her pretty dress was nowhere in sight.

As she sat on a window seat cushion looking like a princess, she held my face in her delicate hand and returned my kiss.

"Happy New Year, Captain," she said.

"Happy New Year to you, beautiful girl," I answered against her lips.

My bones inside my chest felt as though they were going to fracture from the fierce pounding of my heart. I hadn't believed I would ever do what I was about to do...in such a public manner. But, I was.

I went down to the floor on one knee and took both of her hands with both of mine.

A look of surprise came over her face, and then, a quick gasp as she became aware...

"Elaina...I'm going to ask you something. It's a question I meant to ask you six long years ago and I did not. Now, for the second time in our lives, I am prepared to ask the question, and this time, nothing will stop me. You need to know something I've never told you about, because the time has come for you to hear it." I pulled her hands up to my mouth and kissed them both. "You've always made me feel as though the reason I was born...was so I could find you, love you, and that you could love me in return. I believe that with all my heart."

Her eyes filled with tears as she listened. Waiting on me patiently, as was her way.

I pulled out the heart-shaped, sterling-silver box I'd seen her eying in the antique's shop in Washington D.C. and bought, just because I thought she liked it. It reminded me of her. Precious metal, finely wrought into a delicate design, but beautiful, bearing great strength to withstand the tests of time.

I held the box out for her, then popped the clasp that opened it.

"Elaina Morrison, this is our second season. Will you be my Autumn Cherry and bloom for me a second time, marry me, and be my wife? Will you make it possible for me to be able to live a happy life, with you, to achieve the reason for which I was born?"

I stared at what was nestled in the silver heart-shaped box. I looked at him, into the dark eyes I'd always loved—the colour of which matched the dress I was wearing—and answered the question he'd asked me.

"Yes, Neil McManus, I will marry you." I reached a shaking hand out to touch his cheek, his jaw, his lips, and closed my eyes for just a moment to ground myself. "I want to tell you something, too." I opened my eyes and traced over every part of his features, as beautiful now as he'd always been when he was just a boy of seventeen and winked at me over the dinner table. "On the night Ian brought you to us, I fell in love with you and knew I'd just met the boy I would marry someday. For me, it has only ever been…you."

He smiled at me and took the ring out of the silver heart-shaped box. "May I?"

"Yes, you may."

He slipped the aquamarine-blue diamond and platinum ring onto my finger, and then kissed me thoroughly, while still kneeling on the floor. I buried my hands into his hair and held onto my man.

My beautiful, brave, loving, caring man.

I pulled him up to his feet amid loud cheering and congratulatory catcalls, which were coming from well-wishers, who'd apparently been paying attention to what we were doing by the window. Didn't care. Didn't really notice much beyond my beautiful man and the shiny diamond, in glittering blue, on my finger.

Neil scooped me up and carried me out of that party in his arms.

Then, he took me home and made love to me in our bed.

"So…now that I've got your agreement to have me, when will you let me make this merger official?"

She snuggled up against the side of me, the whole warm, naked length of her connecting skin-to-skin with my body, like silver spoons in a drawer. "We just had a merger," she teased.

"That sassy mouth of yours is something I hope never changes, beautiful girl."

"I am making a note of that, Captain, just in case my *sassy* mouth gets me into deep water someday."

I kissed her shoulder right over her tattoo. "You still haven't answered my question, Cherry. When do I get to make you Mrs. McManus?"

She turned her body toward me and held my face as she liked to do. "How long was your final tour in the army?" she asked softly.

"It was ten months."

"I will marry you in ten months, then." She kissed me. "I want to marry you when the autumn cherry trees are having their second bloom in Scotland."

I nodded at her logic, understanding why she'd

chosen that time. And also, because I'm not sure I could have spoken any audible words in that moment, my heart very full and finally at peace.

Then she spoke some more words that I wasn't expecting to hear. Words that just reaffirmed how much love we had for each other and how fate, once again, demanded its due, and this time, worked masterfully in all its wisdom.

"I'm going to give to you...those ten months back. The ones that I took from us six years ago. Ten months of being here with you every night. Ten months of waking up with you every morning. Ten months of our life together, of doing all the beautiful things, and the mundane ones, too. So you will know, that whether it's ten months from now, or ten years, or any amount of years, nothing will change for me, Neil...I will forever be your Cherry Girl."

Epilogue

Ten months later

"You're going to wear a hole in this ancient stone floor if you don't stop pacing like a lunatic. Are you going to sit in the corner and start cradling back and forth, too?"

I gave Ethan my best *sod-off-you-dickhead* look and kept pacing. "Easy for you to say that to me, now that you're already married," I said, truthfully. "I remember how mental you were in that room before you said your vows to Brynne. You would've smoked your Blacks three at a time if we hadn't hidden your stash away where you couldn't find them."

He rolled his eyes and shook his head. "Listen, mate, all will be well in a very short time. You're starting to worry me."

"I feel ill," I said. "I need water."

"I think you need a fucking bottle of Scotch, but really, it's going to be fine."

I nodded and tried to breathe. "What time is it?"

"About two minutes later than the last time you asked." Ethan clapped me on the back and spoke low at my ear. "I saw her in her dress all ready for you when I snuck a peek at my girl in that side room where they're all waiting."

"You saw her? How was she? Did she seem nervous? Did she look worried about anyth—"

"She looked gorgeous and like she couldn't wait to get shackled to you, you big great ape. Do I need to tranquilize you or something?"

"I'll remember this, when Brynne is ready to deliver your baby, and you're a quivering mass of jelly on the floor. Don't worry, I'll return the favour with the offer of tranquilizers."

That did the trick. Shut his fuckin' mouth right up. He rolled his shoulders as if to release tension in his neck, and checked his watch again. "Okay, I'll be honest. The ceremony is a fucking stress-ball of bullshit, and I can't help you even a little bit. The good news is, that in about five more hours, you can start on the wedding night and that part is completely golden." He trolled his palm in the air as if it were gliding, looking like a complete fool.

We both laughed at how stupid we were being and I felt immediately better.

A knock sounded at the door, and the other woman I loved peeked in at us. "Is it all right for me to come in?"

"Of course," I said, bringing her into the room and kissing her on the cheek.

Ethan made some excuse and left us alone. She started fussing with my jacket, brushing at it, adjusting my tie, in that motherly way she'd always had with me.

"You look so handsome, my dear."

"Look at you," I said. "You look like Elaina's sister instead of her mum." She was a beautiful woman, and always had been, but now that she was sober again, the bloom in her skin had returned and she looked healthy.

"Oh, please, we both know that's not true. But really, my darling, I just wanted to have a moment to come and tell you how deeply happy you've made me today, and all the other days since Ian brought you to us. In my heart, I always knew you and Elaina needed to be together in order to find happiness. I always knew how you felt. I know how you used to come to see me and would sneak into her room and touch her things." She smiled at me lovingly. "Some love is just meant to be, and I hope you forgive me for my meddling in bringing the two of you back to each other, but somehow, I think you have."

"Oh, Mum…" I really didn't have words to express my thanks for what she'd done for me. For us. But, I could tell her what it meant to *me*. "You always made me feel like your son. Inside here," I put her hand over my heart, "I am."

"Yes, you are. I have two sons and one daughter, and I love them all so very much."

"I love you, Mum."

"I love you, son." She took a great deep breath and smiled again. I imagine she was thinking of her husband and how he wasn't with her for our wedding. I liked to think that somehow he was. That the family's love for the father, had brought him into the room with us so he could share in the occasion.

"He's here," I said softly.

She smiled and nodded at me, her eyes a little watery, but she put the sadness aside and got down to it like the strong woman she was, and had always been. "Now, I've got Ian in the foyer with Elaina where he's ready to walk her down as soon as the girls go. He'll walk her, then he'll come and stand up with you and Ethan."

"I remember the practice from last night," I said. "I get to seat you in your place first, so shall we, dear Mum?" I held out my arm for her.

"Yes we shall, son." She took my arm and patted my elbow with her hand. "It's well past time for you to marry my daughter."

"Mrs. McManus, your husband is very tired and wishes that all of these people would go away and leave us alone, so he can take you upstairs to our bridal suite and commence with the wedding night."

"Well, I think you've forgotten that most of *these people* are staying here with us in this giant house of yours, and will still be here in the morning when we come down for breakfast."

"Oh, Christ, I'd hoped they wouldn't really take us up on the offer." He nuzzled my neck and inhaled, sending a shiver down my spine.

"I assure you, they have every intention of staying the night here." I laughed.

His shoulders dropped in defeat, and I couldn't help grinning.

"I love your dress. It's very unusual, but so perfect for you, and you look beautiful in it, of course. I especially love the dragonfly right here."

He tapped the dragonfly that was beaded into the blue lace that decorated the back of my white dress.

"I wondered if you might let your tattoo show with your wedding dress," he whispered.
I shook my head. "No. I didn't want it to show. My tattoo is for your eyes alone on this day."

He sat behind me with his chin on my shoulder, letting me feed him small bites of the wedding cake that was not quite as beautiful as it had been earlier. The perfect concoction of sugary cherry blossoms, far too pretty to eat, but eaten it had been. Thankfully, we had many pictures taken by Benny Clarkson, who was doing our wedding photographs. Benny had mad skills and I knew our special day had been captured to the fullest extent, so I didn't mind about the demolished cake. Everyone who mattered to us had come, and it had been the perfect wedding.

"I love that only my eyes will get to see it." He rubbed his thumb up and down my neck, caressing softly, never letting me be out of range for his touch. "I love you…"

"I love you, too, and I love these silver spoons. I think we should feed each other with them every day, don't you?" The gift from Neil to me was two sterling silver spoons with the words, AND THEY LIVED, and, HAPPILY EVER AFTER, stamped into them. He had a knack for finding the unusual and exquisite, and spoilt me every chance he could.

"No doubt, Mrs. McManus."

"So, I have something to give you later," I said.

He groaned. "Oh, well I want it now, please."

I laughed at him. "You don't even know what it is."

He nuzzled me some more. "It's a gift from you, so I *know* I want it right now."

"But what about all these guests that are still here partying like they have absolutely no intention of slowing?" I teased him.

"They won't even know we've left?" he suggested with a brow up.

"I am sure they will notice that the bride and groom are leaving," I said, in a consoling voice.

He sighed and tried again. "How about, I don't bloody care if they notice the bride and groom are leaving?"

"You poor thing, I think I really must take you upstairs and put you to bed."

His face brightened. "You are a good wife, already," he said, with a smile that nearly took my breath away. I would never tire of looking at my beautiful golden man with the chocolate eyes I could drown in.

"Thank you, I plan on being one," I said, reaching for the gift I had prepared just for him. I put it into his hands.

"What's this? My gift?"

I nodded. "It is indeed, Captain. I think you should open it."

"This is the silver heart-shaped box I used when I proposed."

"You're right, it is the same silver box."

He opened the clasp and looked in. He took out what was there. A piece of paper he unfolded and flattened with his hand.

He snapped his head up to me. "Is this right, Cherry?"

"Yes. I stopped taking them three weeks ago."

He stared back down at the paper: my doctor's script for birth control pills with the letters CANCELLED written across. I'd also added in some pink cherry blossom flowers and a blue dragonfly to the best of my drawing ability, which wasn't the greatest, but he would get the idea.

"Well, wife, it appears we have some very important work to do…and I think we need to get started on it right away."

"I agree, Captain. Social etiquette be damned."

"God, you're so utterly perfect, Cherry," he said, as he swept me up into his arms and carried me up the stairs.

Neil had marched us right across the dance floor with the train of my dress trailing behind him, through the crowd of guests who waved us off with cheers and lewd comments, just as soon as they realized what he was doing.

I don't think my man even heard them, or ever noticed that anyone else was still in the room with us.

He only had eyes for his Cherry Girl.

THE END

ABOUT THE AUTHOR

Raine has been reading romance novels since she picked up that first Barbara Cartland paperback at the tender age of thirteen. She thinks it was *The Flame is Love* from 1975. And it's a safe bet she'll never stop reading romance novels because now she writes them too. Granted, Raine's stories are edgy enough to turn Ms. Cartland in her grave, but to her way of thinking, a tall, dark and handsome hero never goes out of fashion. Never! A former teacher turned full- time writer of sexy romance stories, is how she fills her days. Raine has a prince of a husband, and two brilliant sons to pull her back into the real world if the writing takes her too far away. Her sons know she likes to write stories, but have never asked to read any. (Raine is so very grateful about this.) She loves to hear from readers and chat about the characters in her books. You can connect with Raine on Facebook or visit her at **www.RaineMiller.com** to see what she's working on now.

BOOKS BY RAINE MILLER

Naked, The Blackstone Affair, Part 1
All In, The Blackstone Affair, Part 2
Eyes Wide Open, The Blackstone Affair, Part 3
Rare and Precious Things, The Blackstone Affair, Part 4
The Undoing of a Libertine
The Passion of Darius

ACKNOWLEDGEMENTS

*C*herry Girl is a book I never planned to write. When the main characters were set down in my first Blackstone Affair book—*Naked*—I never dreamed that Neil and Elaina would ever have a complete novel and book of their own. Theirs is an amazing and beautiful love story that pulls at the heart, so I am very grateful to be able to share it with you.

Creating the characters in my books is one of the greatest gifts a writer can own. I have also been blessed with the support of friends and colleagues in the writing community who help me in ways that can't really be measured. I do know that I couldn't have created this story without the help of so many people to whom I am greatly indebted.

So, THANK YOU, my wonderful friends, for helping *Cherry Girl* to be born.

My *SC*'s Katie Ashley and Rebecca Lilley, I love you for the amazing and brilliant women that you are. Here's to our triad, and that it never changes. SCOL all the way!

To my beloved street team at **The Blackstone Affair Fan Page**, this book wouldn't even be a book if not for you. Luna, Franzi, Jena, Brandi, Karen, Martha, Jen G., for reading and pimping the books endlessly with your beautiful memes and collages that bring life to the fan page every single day. To Becca Manuel at **Bibliophile Productions** for her generous talents with movie editing software in creating the beautiful book trailer for *Cherry Girl*.

To the madly talented Marya Heiman at **Strong Image Editing** for this amazing cover that still makes me want to weep for how beautiful it is. To Cristina Cappelletti who generously sold the photo rights to me for this book. (She is also the beautiful girl with the gorgeous cherry blossom tattoo on her shoulder.) Sometimes serendipity comes into play, and finding her photograph was one of those times.

To my sweet Marion at **Making Manuscripts** for her support and gentle wisdom in helping me to get this book into shape. You are a priceless gem, darling.

To Cris at **Bookmarked Designs** for formatting this beast for me. I love you and miss your hugs already.

To Trish at **The Occasionalist** for organizing all of the fabulous events I get to travel to and meet the amazing fans that read my books.

And finally, to my family at **Casa de Miller** for loving and supporting me no matter how crazy things get in our lives.

Love is all I got, my dear ones.

Nothing but love and respect for all of you.

xxoo *Raine*

Made in the USA
Lexington, KY
20 September 2014